My Sister's Best Friend

Zoë Tavares Bennett

Foreword to the Second Edition

This is the second edition of *My Sister's Best Friend*, published a year and a half later to include—as promised—bonus content that had been originally included in the Wattpad version of *MSBF* as well as a sneak peek into the sequel, *Best Friends & Their Exes*. The motive for excluding certain bonus content in the first edition of this novel was to prepare for a sequel that would elaborate on one of the bonus chapters. Therefore, I needed time to outline and write that story before including bonus content that would not overlap with the events in the sequel.

I have also had the cover redone by my talented cousin and graphic designer, Alexis Bennett, in order to match the cover for the sequel. For inquiries, contact her at https://alexiscdesign.com.

Another reason for the delay was that I also wrote and published a queer historical retelling of the rise to power of Emperor Augustus at the age of nineteen, called *The*

Sun of God, which is available on Amazon. For more information and updates about new books, blog posts, newsletters, and more, check out my author's website: https://www.zoetavaresbennett.com/

*To my sister, who read this story many years ago
before anyone else knew about it.*

*Thank you for always encouraging me to live
my most authentic life.*

You will always be my best friend, forever.

Contents

1

It was well after midnight when Vera's life changed forever.

She hadn't been doing anything very exciting. Her English teacher had assigned an essay on *The Grapes of Wrath*, which was cumbersome even to Vera, who loved to read. Vera had just wrapped up the first paragraph when the doorbell rang. Breathing a sigh of relief at the welcome interruption, Vera went downstairs.

Halfway down, she stopped, realizing that it was in fact very late at night, and her younger sister Layla was in San Diego for a dance competition, their parents having gone with her.

Vera had never been in a dangerous situation in her eighteen years of life. What if it was someone trying to rob her? Or a psychotic stalker who liked to kidnap teenage girls?

Enough. It's probably just a prank.

But Vera's hands shook as she tiptoed to the kitchen

and grabbed a knife. She had also never stabbed someone, but she hoped it wouldn't come to that.

She neared the door silently. Could a bullet pass through a wooden door? That seemed likely. Vera paused. But what if it was a friend from school, and here she was, opening the door with a knife in hand?

She took a deep breath, shaking the fears from her mind, then opened the door.

"Aspen?" Vera quickly set the knife down on a nearby windowsill, staring at her sister's best friend swaying dangerously in tall heels on the porch steps. Vera pushed up her glasses as if they were causing her visions. "What are you doing here?"

She watched Aspen teeter to the left, her glittery eyelids drooping, before she pitched forward, landing right in Vera's arms, her black hair falling over Vera's shoulders.

"I'm *so* drunk right now," Aspen slurred, then giggled, her arms tightening around Vera's waist and clumsily forcing herself upright. Vera stiffened at the contact. Although she had seen Aspen around a lot because of her sister, they weren't particularly close. In fact, rarely were they ever alone together, so this visit baffled her.

"You're pretty," Aspen whispered, blinking her bright blue eyes up at Vera.

Vera blushed. "Maybe you should lie down."

She dragged Aspen's leaden body towards the living room couch, awkwardly draping her on the cushions. Aspen groaned, then whimpered. Vera was tempted to Google how to deal with a drunk girl, but at that moment Aspen lurched up, clutching her stomach with a grimace.

"I think I'm going to throw up," Aspen said. Vera's eyes widened, her legs freezing in place. Then she thought of her mother's face looking at a vomit-stained couch and quickly ran to the kitchen, grabbing a large bowl. She placed the bowl in Aspen's hands just before she leaned over and puked.

Vera looked away from the bowl, instead reaching out and pulling back Aspen's long hair which had fallen into her face. Aspen gurgled into the bowl, then spit.

"Sorry," Aspen mumbled.

"It's okay," Vera said gently. She grabbed the bowl from Aspen's hands, dumped the contents into the toilet of the downstairs bathroom, then cleaned the bowl in the kitchen sink. Vera returned to a somewhat sobered-up Aspen, placing the cleaned bowl next to the couch. "Just in case you need it again."

Aspen smiled weakly, avoiding Vera's gaze. "Thank you."

Vera stood awkwardly, unsure what to do next. "Do you want to talk?"

Aspen looked up, her eyes wide as if she were surprised Vera was still there. Then her face fell into a sad frown, looking down at her lap. "I'm really tired. Do you think I could crash here for the night?"

Vera flushed with embarrassment. Of course Aspen didn't want to talk. She probably got drunk in order *not* to talk. "Sure. You can sleep in Layla's room. She's in San Diego."

"I know." Aspen smiled forcibly.

"Right." Vera looked around as if the surrounding furniture might help her. When the room stayed stubbornly silent, Vera grabbed the bowl and reached out a hand, which Aspen took to pull herself up. On her feet, Aspen quickly lost balance, and Vera's hands shot out to hold Aspen up.

"Come on, I'll help you," Vera said. Aspen nodded reluctantly, then they struggled up the stairs to Layla's room.

Inside the room was dark, the blinds closed on the windows, and the bed unmade. Aspen sat down on the edge of the bed to pull her heels off, then crawled into the middle of the blankets, drawing them close around her. Vera placed the bowl on the floor beside the bed and then stood awkwardly at the door.

"Thank you. Again," Aspen said, avoiding Vera's gaze.

"It was no problem. Really." Vera gave her a small smile, then turned and left, closing the door behind her.

She was halfway to her room when she realized Aspen would want medication and water when she woke up, so Vera quickly went to the kitchen to retrieve two ibuprofen and a glass of water.

Vera opened the door to Layla's room slowly. On the bed, Aspen snored softly, already passed out. Her shimmering dress was hitched up over her hip, revealing red lace. Vera averted her widening eyes, placing the water and pills on the nightstand.

Suddenly Aspen muttered something. Vera glanced at her, but she was still asleep, her black hair spilling on the white pillow like a pool of ink. Vera let out a sigh of relief.

Aspen murmured unintelligibly again, this time twisting around, which only brought the dress up more. Vera blushed involuntarily, then carefully lifted the blankets up to Aspen's chest.

Vera had her hand on the doorknob when Aspen spoke.

"Vera?" Aspen's voice sounded groggy. Vera froze, for some reason feeling caught. She tried to say something but the words stayed stuck in her throat. "Please don't tell Layla I was here."

Vera stared at Aspen's creased forehead and the wide,

round blue eyes that wavered with a shame that Vera was not expecting to see.

"I won't," Vera promised. She returned to her room, weighed down from exhaustion and confusion, yawning just as her head hit the pillow.

2

Morning came bright and early, Saturday with it. Vera woke up late, leaving her warm bed grudgingly to eat breakfast. She poured a bowl of cereal, then grabbed the milk, before she realized what had been nagging at her since she opened her eyes.

Aspen.

Hurriedly—Layla and her parents were supposed to arrive any minute now—she shot up the stairs towards Layla's room.

Vera didn't bother with being quiet, swinging the door open, mouth opening to tell Aspen she had to leave, when she saw the empty bed, the imprint of a body already fading.

"Vera?"

She whirled around, half-expecting to find Aspen leaning against the wall with those blue eyes sharply assessing her, but instead Vera blinked and it was Layla, her arms crossed, a brow raised.

"What are you doing in my room?" Layla asked sharply.

"You're back!" Vera exclaimed, diverting the attention from her, walking over to Layla and hugging her. Layla rolled her eyes but hugged her back. "How'd it go?"

Layla bit her lip, and Vera almost changed the subject thinking she had done badly in the competition when Layla grinned. "We won our division!" Layla squealed.

Vera gasped. "That's amazing! We have to celebrate."

Layla nodded, then narrowed her eyes, and Vera knew she wouldn't get away with it. "You still didn't explain why you were in my room, looking all guilty."

Vera frowned. "I don't look guilty."

"Don't change the subject," Layla said.

Vera sighed, trying to come up with an excuse that seemed reasonable. "I need a sports bra. I'm going for a run and all mine need to be washed."

Partially true. Vera tried to run a few times a week, and besides, asking for clothes was not unusual between them. In fact, it was constantly occurring, being only two years apart. But Vera had sports bras in her room. She just hoped Layla wouldn't go snooping later.

"Oh. Sure, let me get it for you," Layla replied, pushing past Vera toward her closet. She dug her hands into a mound of unorganized clothes, finally pulling out a gray

Nike sports bra. She tossed it to Vera, and Vera was almost out the door when Layla called her name, causing her heart to skip a beat.

"Yes?"

"I forgot to tell you. You're supposed to take me and Aspen to the fair today." She smirked. "Perks of winning a dance competition and having an older sister who can drive and has no friends."

"I have friends!" Vera protested, before realizing what Layla had said. "And I'm not chauffeuring you anywhere."

She fled downstairs to confront their parents before Layla could stop her.

"Mom! Dad! This is not fair. I am not Layla's personal driver," Vera said as she entered the living room. Her parents were both sitting on the couch, and their heads hardly turned from the news playing on the television.

"Vera, it's just for today," her mom said distractedly. Vera crossed her arms and looked at her dad. He just looked at her over his shoulder with an apologetic smile.

"I'll only do it if you give me money to buy a book," Vera said.

Her mom shook her head. "You don't need any more books."

"You should be happy I'm not buying drugs!"

Her mom rolled her eyes, grabbing her purse. "Fine. Just this once."

Vera smiled triumphantly and then walked over to her mom. But before she could snatch the twenty dollars from her mom's hand, she held it away. "But only after you take them," her mom added.

Vera groaned. She returned to her room and quickly changed into jogging shorts, shaking her head as she pulled on Layla's gray sports bra and a large T-shirt. She checked the time. Almost midday. Vera quickly took off her glasses and put in her contacts, blinking until they felt comfortable.

Vera called to her parents as she walked out of the door. "Going for a run! Be back soon." She slammed the door and took off before anyone replied.

Once her legs caught a rhythm and her breath quickened, Vera felt better. Besides school and books, the only other thing she really understood was running. It was one foot in front of the other, going for as long as she wanted. Competition against another team confused Vera. She had run track and cross country her freshman year, but she hated the idea of being timed or ranked, so she didn't join the next year.

She reached home thirty minutes later, her hair stuck to her temples and her body humming. The moment she opened the front door, Layla's shouts bombarded her.

"Where were you? It's almost one and the fair closes at nine!"

"Calm down Layla, I'll get ready," Vera said, pushing Layla away and moving towards the kitchen for a glass of water.

"Vera?" a voice asked in surprise. The arm reaching for a glass froze in midair. Vera turned around, trying to school her lips into a smile, but they stayed slightly parted.

Aspen was sitting on an arm of the couch, blue eyes sharp and focused on Vera. She wasn't wearing her silver dress or red lace anymore, instead snug in tight jeans and a red crop top. Vera couldn't help thinking back to last night, which felt like ages ago.

"You look so different without glasses," Aspen said. "I don't think I've ever seen you without them."

"I only take them off to run." Vera didn't know why her cheeks were heating up, but it was like Aspen was looking at her differently.

Next to them, Layla sighed irritably. "Can you hurry up? We need to go."

Vera rolled her eyes, but filled up her glass anyways, heading upstairs. She could just make out Aspen telling her sister to chill out. Vera bit her lip to prevent a smile.

After showering, she pulled on a pair of mom jeans and a white button-up shirt, then went downstairs. Aspen and Layla were laughing on the couch, looking at something on their phones, when Vera stepped on the landing. She watched as Aspen smiled, her glossy lips curving, and her blue eyes looking skyward.

Vera shook the thought away. "Let's go. I'm ready."

Layla got up from the couch. "Finally." *So dramatic.*

Aspen got up with her eyes on Vera, who turned away before the other girl could see her blush.

"So, Mom said you had to stay with us at the fair. She said something about not buying you a book?" Layla mentioned without really looking at Vera, her attention fixated on what she was typing on her phone.

Vera's gaze unintentionally wandered to Aspen, who raised a brow. Her face felt hot, and she quickly turned away, opening the door. Then she unlocked the small white car parked in their driveway, and Layla hopped in the back excitedly. Aspen followed with her usual effortless confidence. Vera slid into the driver's seat, turning the key in the ignition.

Layla reached forward to grab the aux cord, connecting it to her phone. Justin Bieber spilled out of the speakers and Vera groaned.

"Not this," Vera said. Layla muttered something and

Aspen stifled a laugh. There was a scuffle in the back seat, and Vera forced herself not to look back at them. Suddenly the song cut off to the lead singer of Arctic Monkeys and his drawling British accent.

Vera smiled. She loved Alex Turner.

"Really, Aspen?" Layla asked, but she did not change the song. *Aspen liked Arctic Monkeys too?* Vera looked up to the rearview mirror in surprise, where her eyes met Aspen's like she knew Vera was going to look. Vera settled her gaze back on the road.

Every time Aspen looked at her, Vera felt like she was missing something. W*as it about last night? Did she want to talk to Vera? Or was this all in her imagination?*

They reached the fair in fifteen minutes, three of those spent just trying to find parking.

"It's like the whole city is here," Layla said, looking around at the surging crowds entering the fairgrounds. The fair took place annually for three days a few weeks before spring break. There were rides that shot screaming teenagers up into the sky and numerous booths that displayed prizes like stuffed animals and fake lightsabers. Vera didn't particularly like fairs or festivals, but she enjoyed eating the popcorn and churros they sold and going on the occasional ride that didn't flip upside down.

But Layla and Aspen were not here for the rides or the

booths. They were here for the boys.

As if they were magnets, several boys came sauntering up to Layla and Aspen. Vera knew Layla had some sort of thing going on with a boy at school, so she acted reservedly as the boys hugged them. Aspen, on the other hand, flirted shamelessly with a few of them, laughing and smiling and placing a hand on their arm.

Why did Vera care?

Vera walked over to a nearby table, sitting down with her back to Layla and Aspen. She felt confused, like she had taken a wrong step. What was it about Aspen that suddenly had Vera questioning herself?

She turned without realizing it. Aspen was looking at her casually as she talked with a tall, blonde boy, who Vera recognized in belated embarrassment as her classmate in English. Vera turned around, her stomach twisting with conflicting emotions. Why was Aspen looking at her?

Before she knew it, jealousy shot through her. Vera had a few close friends at school, but she never had a boyfriend, just a clumsy kiss with some boy that she didn't even like. And it was once. Vera knew from Layla that Aspen was quite popular, and had a boy interested in her every weekend, sometimes two. For Vera, that seemed an impossible feat, as well as unnecessary.

Vera almost turned to look once more when someone sat in front of her. A boy. What did he want? Vera reproached herself for thinking it. If she wanted a boyfriend, she would need an open mind. And this boy was cute, with curly copper hair, tan skin, and freckles dotting the bridge of his nose. Vera thought she recognized him from school.

"Is this not your scene?" he asked. Vera frowned, then smiled. How did Aspen keep it on?

"No, not really," Vera said, looking down at the table, blushing even though it was just a normal question. When she looked up, the boy was grinning, like he thought she was endearing.

"Same. But I was forced to come," he said, gesturing behind Vera. She turned and saw the group of boys talking with Layla and Aspen. An unexpected laugh escaped Vera's lips as she faced him.

"Me too." She decided that she liked this boy's smile. It brought a knowing sparkle into his eyes that flipped Vera's stomach. He looked behind her again.

"Those your friends?" he asked.

Vera shook her head, and she felt unreasonably embarrassed. "My sister and her friend." And when she noticed his confusion, added, "I have the car."

Understanding dawned on his face, and he smiled

again, as bright as the sunshine filtering through his curls. "I'm Will by the way. Actually, it's William, but I like Will." He stretched out a hand and Vera took it, and she liked how her hand fit in his.

"Vera. And it's not short for anything."

Will smiled, amused. "Nice to meet you."

This time it was easier to smile. "Yeah, nice to meet you too."

Vera didn't really know what to say, but she was saved from scrambling for a conversation starter when Aspen's voice came from behind her.

"Vera."

She turned to see Aspen standing behind her, a manicured hand on her hips, shiny red nails glittering in the sun. Vera squinted up at Aspen's locked jaw and glinting eyes that flickered from Vera to Will. "Layla told me to tell you that we're going to a booth. And you need to watch over us, right?"

Vera glanced at Will, who raised a brow. "I can join you, if you want."

"Sure," Vera said, then looked at his friends uneasily. "Is that okay with them?"

Will laughed. "If it means they get to hang out with your sister, I'm sure they'll be more than fine with it."

Vera smiled. The boys surrounding her sister did seem

giddy, their chests puffed out, but still trying to act casual.

"And you don't want to hang out with my sister?" Vera asked jokingly. Will shook his head, and was about to speak when Aspen cut him off.

"Enough flirting," she said irritably. "Everyone's waiting."

Vera shot her a bemused glance, the blush on her cheeks fading from the confusion at Aspen's tone, but Aspen was already walking back to Layla and the group of boys.

Will kept stride next to her as Vera followed them. "So…you go to Hilltop right?" Will asked.

"Yeah. Senior." Vera pushed up her glasses, looking around at the milling crowds around the booths. "Are you a junior like my sister?"

"I'm an old junior." Will flashed a dazzling smile. "Turning eighteen on June first."

"I turned eighteen in December," Vera said. She smiled secretly when she caught that look of respect in Will's eyes.

"Six months difference." Will winked. "I've always had a thing for older women."

Vera choked on a laugh as Will laughed too, giving himself away. This flirting might just give her a heart attack. Will, on the other hand, had a smug smile on his face.

"You're impossible," Vera said. Will only laughed.

They continued across the fair, following the group of boys surrounding Layla and Aspen like bees around honey. Vera was surprised she enjoyed talking with Will and enduring his flirting, and it would have been perfect if Aspen hadn't been practically glaring at both of them whenever she had the chance. Even Will noticed, and he asked Vera why Aspen was looking at them.

"I think she's just stressed," Vera said worriedly. Will looked unconvinced but they didn't bring her up again. Soon the night snuck up on them, and before Vera knew it, the fair was closing in half an hour, and Layla and Aspen were ready to leave.

"I'll text you," Will said quietly to Vera, causing her to blush yet again. She had never been that quick getting to know anyone, let alone a boy, and a cute one at that. When Will had asked for her number, she had frozen mid-stride and nearly face-planted if not for Will catching her by the arm, which only made her more flustered. That ordeal rewarded them with a particularly vicious look from Aspen, zone of many that Vera still could not understand. Did she like Will?

But that was impossible. Didn't she have a boyfriend?

"Are we leaving or not?" Aspen asked, looking at Layla,

but it was clearly meant for Vera.

Layla cast a bewildered glance at Aspen, but then she crossed her arms at Vera. "Yeah, Vera, let's go."

Vera rolled her eyes, then turned to say goodbye to Will. He was already there, enveloping Vera in a hug. For a moment, Vera was engulfed by the faint smell of cologne and the pleasant heat that seemed to seep into her skin. And then it was gone, and Layla was dragging her away by the arm. She turned to see one of Will's friends pat him on the back and say something in a low tone, causing Will's cheeks to bloom red.

Vera smiled to herself as she got in the car and pulled out of the parking lot. Behind her Layla plugged in her phone and Aspen glared out the window.

"So you seemed to be talking a lot with Will," Layla said over the pop music gently playing from the speakers.

Vera felt herself blush at the mention of his name. She tried not to smile. "He's really nice," she admitted.

Layla could barely contain a squeal. "And cute!" Aspen scoffed and Layla turned on her accusingly. "What is up with you today? You were sulking all day."

"Nothing. You were just flirting with all those guys and saying Will is cute when you practically have a boyfriend," Aspen said.

The car went silent. For some reason, Vera felt that

Aspen wasn't telling the truth.

"Are you kidding me Aspen? That's rich coming from you," Layla shot back venomously.

Vera knew a fight was coming now. She never understood how they could fight over such trivial things. Vera and her friends rarely fought, though they weren't as close as Layla and Aspen were, who had known each other since elementary school when they used to take dance classes together. They were both vibrant, outgoing girls who loved to party and hang out with their friends all the time. Vera preferred the coziness of her bed to a house party, and her idea of fun was reading a book.

"And what's that supposed to mean?" Aspen asked angrily.

Layla didn't hesitate. "You hook up all the time. You've practically run out of guys at school because you've been with all of them. Not to mention Kyle."

Vera couldn't help it. She looked up at the rearview mirror. Aspen glanced up at the same time and their eyes met. A shadow flickered across Aspen's face. Vera quickly looked away, unsure if the shame she had just seen in Aspen's eyes was a trick of the light. Could it be that Aspen was ashamed? And was that because of Vera?

"I haven't been with all of them and you know it," Aspen said. She had lost her acidity from before and her words sounded more miserable than truly angry. Layla let out a sigh and remained resolutely silent for the rest of the drive.

Vera parked in the driveway of their house, then walked towards the door. Layla followed, but Aspen stayed on the sidewalk, rapidly typing something on her phone. Vera looked at Layla in question.

"She's calling an Uber," Layla said coldly. Vera hesitated, then decided this had nothing to do with her, and besides, Aspen hadn't been very pleasant to Vera either. They entered the house, shutting the door behind them.

"Oh, hey girls," their mom called from the kitchen. She came over to them in an apron, her graying brown hair tied back.

"Hey Mom," Vera said. Layla just stomped upstairs to her room.

Their mom's eyes followed Layla as she stormed down the hall, followed by a slammed door. She raised a brow at Vera. "What's wrong with her?"

"Got in a fight with Aspen," Vera explained.

"Ah, I see." Her mom walked back to the kitchen, and Vera followed, leaning against the counter until her mom noticed. "Dinner's not going to be ready for another thirty minutes, you know."

"I know," Vera said. She stayed where she was until her

mom glanced at her while rummaging in a cupboard.

"Why are you staring at me like that? Don't you have something else to do?" her mom asked.

Vera waited expectantly. When her mom sighed in exasperation, Vera held out her hand. "Money for the book."

Her mom blinked at her, then started laughing, pulling the twenty dollars out of her pocket and handing the money to Vera. "I'm gonna go broke at this rate."

Vera smiled sweetly. "At least it's not drugs!"

Her mom rolled her eyes. Vera fled to her room before her mom could ask for help with dinner, satisfied with her reward.

3

*T**hud thud thud.*

Vera looked up from her book and towards the noise. It was the front door. Her parents were out, her mom buying groceries, her dad at work, and Layla at dance practice. Maybe it was just a delivery.

Thud thud thud.

"I'm coming!" Vera shouted, muttering under her breath about how impatient people were these days. She opened the door and was immediately hit with a wave of *déjà vu.* Standing on the porch with a worried expression was Aspen, her fist poised to knock again. She lowered her arm when she saw Vera.

"Layla isn't home," Vera said automatically.

"I know," Aspen said, nervously tugging at the hem of her sweatshirt. "I came to talk to you."

"Oh…Why?"

Aspen avoided Vera's gaze, staring at her shoes instead.

"I…I know that I wasn't the nicest yesterday," Aspen started cautiously. "Lately I've been feeling a bit overwhelmed. So, I'm sorry about yesterday."

Vera still didn't understand anything that was happening, yesterday or today, but the apology alone warmed her heart. But then she remembered her sister. "I mean, I appreciate the apology, but you should really be apologizing to Layla." Vera watched closely as Aspen's face hardened, and she frowned.

"I didn't come just to apologize, actually," Aspen said. "I wanted to talk about Friday night. Or Saturday morning, technically…" Aspen trailed off. For the first time, she looked truly awkward, glancing at Vera before darting her eyes towards the ground.

"Oh." Vera paused. "You can come in if you want." She walked back into the house.

Aspen hesitated at the doorway before walking in and closing the door behind her. The click of the lock echoed through the tense silence. Vera led them to the couch, feeling eyes burn into her back as she sat down. Aspen gingerly sat down on the edge of the couch a respectful distance away.

"So…what about it did you want to talk about?" Vera asked, unsure of where to begin.

Aspen bit her lip. "I just want you to know that I

normally don't get drunk like that." Vera raised a brow, startled at the sudden confession. "And I haven't been with all the guys at school either."

Aspen stared at Vera anxiously. What did Aspen want from her?

"Okay?" Vera asked slowly. Aspen ran a hand down her face, blowing out a breath.

"I just…don't want you to see me that way. Like some dumb girl that parties all the time and gets drunk and doesn't care about consequences," Aspen said.

"W-what?" Vera stammered, in shock at this random honesty. Where was all this coming from? Aspen's eyes widened with fear, and Vera rushed to amend her reaction. "I mean, of course I don't see you that way. Everyone has their bad nights every once in a while. Why are you so worried?"

Aspen's shoulders relaxed slightly, but she still seemed a bit torn. Her blue eyes were dark and heavy when she looked up at Vera again, and hesitated as if carefully thinking of how to phrase what she wanted to say next.

"Did I say anything, or do anything, that night?" Aspen asked cautiously.

Vera was perplexed by the question. Was Aspen worried she told her someone's secret? Like Layla's?

"I don't think so," Vera said, letting her mind wander

to that night. "You just showed up at the door, and you were pretty drunk. You fell, so I had to catch you. Then you said I was pretty." Vera flushed, not knowing why she had said that. Aspen's eyes snapped up to Vera's so she continued quickly. "I led you to the couch. And you threw up. Then I helped you up to Layla's room and you passed out. You said something about not telling Layla. In the morning, you were gone." Vera half-smiled. "I'm glad you took the Advil. Layla would have been a bit more suspicious if she saw those."

Aspen smiled shyly. "Thanks for that. Thanks for everything, actually."

"Oh, it's on big deal," Vera said. Aspen's smile lit up her eyes, and Vera blushed.

Aspen opened her mouth to say something but froze when the front door lock opened. Vera and Aspen stared at each other for a split second before Aspen grabbed her purse and quickly pulled out a white cord, dropping it in her lap. A phone charger.

"Thanks again," Aspen said loudly, taking the charger and walking towards the door, where Layla and her mom were just entering. Layla's head shot up at the sound of her best friend, her eyes instantly narrowing.

"What are you doing here?" Layla asked angrily. Aspen barely spared her a glance, showing her the charger and opening the door.

"I forgot this yesterday," Aspen said breezily, and she left the house before Layla could say another word. Layla swung her hard gaze to Vera, who shrugged. After a string of unladylike words aimed at Aspen left Layla's mouth, she marched upstairs and slammed her door shut.

"Layla!" their mom exclaimed, shocked by the sudden exchange and the resulting curses. She looked at Vera. "Do I even want to know?"

"Probably not," Vera said, then returned to her own room to catch up on homework, grateful for the excuse to have some peace and quiet.

4

The beginning of the school week started so normally that Vera had completely forgotten about the strange occurrences of the weekend. That is, until Will walked around the corner of the hallway with his group of friends, coming straight towards Vera. She was on her way to Physics, which was unfortunately her first class that Wednesday morning. When Will saw Vera, his face lit up, and he said something to his friends before jogging over to her.

Vera was so stunned that she froze in the middle of the hallway and was clipped in the shoulder by a student rushing past. She barely found her balance before Will came up and hugged her.

"Good morning?" Vera said, but it came out more as a question, causing Will to laugh. His chest vibrated against hers and she felt a rush of excitement that he thought she was funny.

"It's definitely better now that I've seen you," Will

said, stepping back. Vera must have looked so disheveled, her hair wild and her cheeks blushing. "I didn't actually expect to see you at school. You must be in all those advanced classes, huh?"

"What class do you have?" Vera asked before he could come up with more ways to make her blush.

Will pulled on the straps of his backpack, a smug smile on his face. "AP Lang."

"I took that last year," Vera said, smiling triumphantly. Will laughed again, and it was so goofy he had her laughing with him. He shook his head with a smile, his copper curls bouncing against his cheeks.

"No need to rub it in," Will said, a hand pressed against his heart jokingly. "What class do you have next?"

"Physics."

Will had the decency to grimace. "Good luck with that."

"Thanks. I'll need all the luck I can get."

Then they parted ways to class, Vera still humming and warm, as if Will's presence had woken her up. For the rest of the day, Vera felt alive and focused, rather than her usual tired self. She was practically whistling as she walked inside her house, placing her car keys on the trinket tray near the door.

"At least someone's happy today," Layla muttered

moodily, before disappearing to her room, most likely to Facetime her friends. Vera grabbed an apple from the kitchen before heading upstairs as well.

Once she was inside her room, Vera threw her backpack on the floor and then jumped on her bed. Just as she felt comfortable under a heap of blankets, her phone rang. Groaning, Vera crawled to her backpack, struggling to find her phone among the books and binders.

"Hello?"

Silence.

"Hello? Who is this?" Vera asked again. She nearly brought the phone down to hang up when a soft voice spoke.

"Vera?" It was Aspen. At the sound of her voice, Vera sat up straight, her heart thudding loudly in her chest. "Are you there?"

"Yes, I'm here," Vera said, her voice sounding far away. "Why are you calling me?"

She hadn't meant to sound rude, but she was just so shocked. Aspen remained silent for a few moments.

Suddenly Aspen asked, "Can I come over?"

"No!" Vera exclaimed loudly, before lowering her voice. "Layla's at home."

Aspen let out a breath on the other line. "Can you pick me up from my house? We can figure out where to go from there."

"Why?" Vera asked. "Why me? Why not Layla, or some other friend?"

"Usually I would talk to Layla about this, but she and I aren't on the best of terms right now." She hesitated as if struggling to come up with the right words. "I don't know why, but I feel like I can talk to you. Like you would understand."

"Oh." She was not exactly surprised by this. Layla and her parents said the same thing to her, and she often found herself giving advice to them. But Aspen was different. She was not direct family. Not even a friend, really.

"I totally get it if you're busy," Aspen said. "Or if it's too awkward for you. I'm just...I need someone to talk to." Vera could detect the urgency underlying her words, and Vera knew she wouldn't be able to turn Aspen down, not when she sounded like this.

"What's your address?" Vera asked. Then she grabbed her keys and made for the door.

Vera pulled up to Aspen's house fifteen minutes later. Aspen was standing in the shadow of a tree, looking around nervously, hitching up her small black purse on her shoulder. Her signature color must be red because today she wore red shorts and a temporary tattoo of a cherry, probably bought at the fair, was pasted on her left hip.

She did a right turn signal, then stopped in front of the house. Aspen made her way towards the car.

"Thanks for picking me up," Aspen said once she got settled in the passenger seat, fiddling with the zipper of her purse.

"Where do you want to go?" Vera asked.

"How about we go to Rosemary Park and then walk around the garden?"

Vera couldn't help thinking how romantic that would be. Maybe she should invite Will another time, then almost laughed at the idea. Will wouldn't want to go to a garden! And if he did, it would be because he knew Vera loved gardens and would ask her on a date.

"That sounds great," Vera confessed, then merged into traffic.

Aspen stayed silent for most of the drive, looking out the window. She asked once if Vera wanted music, and when Vera said yes, Aspen turned on the radio, fiddling with the stations from time to time.

The Rosemary Park sign loomed into view, and Vera pulled into the parking lot. Now that they were here,

Vera's stomach turned in anticipation. She stole a glance towards Aspen, who was tapping on the passenger door nervously.

Vera parked, then hesitated. She looked to her right and saw that Aspen hadn't made a move to get out of the car either. Vera would never admit it out loud, but for a moment, it felt like they were going on an awkward first date.

"The gardens?" Aspen asked.

Vera nodded, and they hastily got out of the car. They followed the signs that read 'Garden' until they found themselves walking between rows upon rows of flower bushes, some with red roses, yellow tulips, and purple jasmine, bees buzzing past and the sun peeking behind white, puffy clouds.

"Do you want to sit there?" Aspen asked, pointing to a nearby bench positioned under the shade of a large willow tree.

"Sure." Vera didn't want to have to make eye contact while talking about whatever Aspen needed to talk about, but she sat down anyway. She watched as Aspen twisted a strand of black hair around her finger. "So, what did you want to talk about?"

Aspen looked up, startled, before laughing awkwardly, though her eyes were saddened. "This is a lot harder to say randomly," she admitted. "Well, my dad has cancer."

Vera tried hard not to gasp. "What type of cancer?"

She didn't really know how to handle this type of thing, especially since she had never really lost anyone close to her before. Aspen didn't seem to notice anything wrong with her question. In fact, her shoulders lowered in relief.

"I'm glad you asked that instead of saying sorry or something," Aspen said. "He has pancreatic cancer. They caught it in stage two, but the doctors are still worried about it. I just can't believe he has it. Like you hear all those stories about people having cancer, but you never think it's gonna happen to someone so close, you know? And I feel so bad because I've been such a horrible daughter. The day I found out about my dad I got so drunk I blacked out and my friends called my mom and she was so worried and angry. She grounded me after that, of course, with no friends allowed except Layla. And now I've ruined that too. I mean, that night I came to your house because Kyle dumped me after I kissed—" Aspen broke off, flushed with bright, misted eyes. Vera didn't say anything, all the possible things to say stuck in her throat. "Total TMI. Sorry," Aspen said, embarrassed.

Vera didn't know how it happened, but suddenly her hand was reaching out and grabbing hold of Aspen's. Their fingers laced together, but Vera didn't let herself think about it. "Don't be sorry. None of this is your fault. Growing up is about making mistakes and learning from them, and dealing with all the awful things life throws at us. It's okay to let it all out sometimes."

When she stopped, Vera saw Aspen's eyes shining with tears. For a moment, terror gripped Vera's chest at the realization that she might have said something inconsiderate, but then without letting go of Vera's hand, Aspen leaned forward and hugged Vera tightly.

"Thank you," Aspen whispered. Vera could hardly think, the only thought in her mind that Aspen smelled nice, like strawberries and the sharper edge of a faint perfume.

"You're welcome," Vera said, a blush heating her face. When they parted, Aspen stood up, and since their hands were still laced together, Vera stood up with her.

"I also think I'm going to apologize to Layla. Do you think you could take me with you when you go back to your house?" Aspen asked, and when she saw Vera's face, added, "We'll just tell her you saw me walking a few blocks away and decided to give me a lift."

Vera was still too stunned by the hug to do anything but agree.

They started walking back to the car. After a few steps, Vera realized they were still holding hands. Suddenly, all she could think about was how nicely their hands fitted together. Vera knew this was strange, that something was going on here, and that Aspen keeping her hand in Vera's had to mean something too.

She was just afraid to name it.

All too soon they reached her car. Aspen stopped, looking down at their entwined hands. She cleared her throat but didn't say anything. Vera watched Aspen smile faintly, and something fluttered in Vera's chest.

Then Aspen's hand left hers and she slid into the passenger seat. Vera got in the car, trying to conceal her trembling hands as she gripped the steering wheel.

5

"Vera? Are you with us?"

Vera's head snapped up at the teacher saying her name. All eyes turned to her. She had been caught daydreaming. *Again.* The first time was halfway through first period. The second time happened five minutes later, to which the teacher asked if she was feeling well. Second period she had a history exam. If it hadn't been on such easy material, Vera would have failed it. And now this.

"I'm sorry," Vera said, flushing at the disappointment on her teacher's face. With a stern look, the teacher continued her lecture.

The class could not have gone any slower. For the first time, Vera understood how torturous school could be. She glanced at the clock. Five more minutes.

Despite herself, Vera's mind began to wander again, like it had been all day, to strawberries and perfume, to cherry tattoos and laced hands, to long black hair and red shorts. She wondered when they were going to talk again. *If* they were going to talk again, Vera corrected. That was probably a one-time thing, and everything would go back to normal. The thought turned Vera's stomach, and she could've shouted for joy when the bell rang.

Out in the hall, Vera met up with her two close friends, Piper and Jane. Piper's flaming red hair stood out against the crowd of students as she made her way to Vera, a quiet, serious-faced Jane in tow.

"So have you heard?" Piper said once Vera was in earshot, linking their arms together. Piper loved to gossip, and always had something to tell, usually accompanied by a funny story. Vera didn't usually care about gossip, but Piper could make anything sound interesting.

"Heard what?" Vera asked. Piper's mouth fell open dramatically. Jane snorted next to them. She was always cynical when it came to basically everything.

"Sydney and Jack broke up last night!" Piper exclaimed.

Vera did her part and gasped. It actually was somewhat surprising, considering Sydney and Jack were the star couple at Hilltop High, and everyone thought they would get married. Well, everyone except Jane.

"High school relationships never last," Jane said.

Piper glared at her. "Some do. Anyways, there's a rumor going on that Sydney cheated on him a while ago." Vera's eyes widened as they took a seat at their usual lunch table. Piper paused for dramatic effect. "And people say it was with a girl."

Jane rolled her eyes, twirling one of her waist-length braids between her fingers as if she were already bored of the conversation. "So what?"

But Vera's heart stuttered in her chest, and not in a good way. She forced her face to act normal and sound as disinterested as Jane. "It was probably a dare or something. Or a joke."

Piper smiled, her eyes lighting up, as if Vera had said exactly what she wanted to hear. "But that's the thing. Sydney is bi."

"Really?" Vera asked.

"Yeah. How did you not know that?" Piper sounded offended. Now Vera rolled her eyes.

"Not everyone cares about gossip like you do," Jane said. Now it was Piper's turn to roll her eyes, but Vera suspected this was because Jane was dating a very attractive basketball player and never bragged about it, of which Piper was very jealous.

"Whatever," Piper said hurriedly. "People want to know who the other girl was. They think it was someone from Hilltop." She looked around suspiciously. "Who do you think it was?"

Vera had no clue, and would prefer to change the subject. Would it be too obvious if she asked Jane about their math homework?

"Probably Principal Weber. Scratch that. Definitely Principal Weber."

Vera looked up at the familiar voice, and Piper made a weird sound as she chewed. Will was standing directly in front of the sun, forming a yellow halo around his curly hair.

"Hey Will," Vera said, blushing when Piper sent her a look that meant she would have to explain later. Even Jane looked confused.

Will grinned. "Nice day isn't it? Wanna hang out later? Maybe see a movie?"

Vera felt her heart beat just a bit faster. Will wanted to hang out. After school. Piper gave her a not-so-subtle jab with her elbow.

"Oh, yes. Of course."

Will's grin stretched wider, if possible. Vera felt that warm feeling spread throughout her chest again.

"I'll text you later, then," Will said, walking away backward, then giving them a wave before turning and rejoining his friends at another table.

Piper turned on her immediately, her voice so high it was nearly a screech. "How do you know Will?!" Vera winced, and Jane shook her head in exasperation. "Explain yourself!"

"Okay, *mom,* just calm down," Vera said. Jane laughed. "I met him at the fair last weekend. His friends know Layla."

"Vera, you are full of surprises today," Piper said, narrowing her eyes in mock seriousness.

Jane raised a brow. "What other surprises did Vera have?"

Vera laughed, but Piper only crossed her arms defiantly. She couldn't help thinking about Aspen.

Oh, Jane, you have no idea.

When Vera opened the front door, she heard Aspen's laugh. *Guess they must have made up then,* Vera thought. She was right. Layla and Aspen were relaxing on the couch, Layla's legs thrown over Aspen's. They must have walked here from school, or someone else drove them. Vera had assumed that when Layla texted her to drive alone, she was going to Aspen's house.

Layla looked up from the couch to Vera and smiled.

"Hey sis."

Vera stood near the stairs, hands awkwardly fiddling with the straps of her backpack. "Someone's in a good mood." Layla rolled her eyes, but she still smiled. Then before she could change her mind, Vera added, "I could've driven you guys from school."

"I know! I told Aspen that but she insisted that her mom drive us," Layla said, playfully poking Aspen's leg.

Vera glanced at Aspen, but she was looking down at her phone, her hair hiding her face. It was suddenly difficult to breathe, and Vera tried to mask the hurt and disappointment that blossomed in her stomach with a small smile.

"Well, next time," Vera said. She glanced at Aspen one last time, but she was saying something to Layla, and her expression didn't give away what she was thinking. Vera went up to her room, shutting the door.

Why was she so bothered by this? Aspen didn't owe Vera anything. And even if Aspen were to say something, what could she say that didn't sound suspicious in front of Layla? Vera was overreacting.

Suddenly she was hit with the realization that she might have a sort of…crush on Aspen. It's probably just admiration. Nothing serious or real. Nothing like *that*.

Vera took a deep breath, then let it out, trying to clear

her thoughts.

Beep. Vera's phone vibrated in her backpack, and she took it out with her stomach flipping. Could it be Aspen?

It was Will. Her disappointment faded with the excitement for Will's text.

Will: Have you seen Dunkirk yet?

Vera: No…

Will: Want to meet up at the movie theater on East Avenue? Dunkirk plays at 7:30 pm.

Vera: I'll be there.

Will: That's all I ask, but a hug would be awesome too.

Vera: Don't push it.

Will: Wouldn't dream of it.

Twenty minutes past seven, Vera got out of her car and walked towards the movie theater. She waited outside, not exactly nervous, but definitely excited at the thought of seeing Will. A few minutes later, a silver minivan pulled up in front, and Will hopped out of the passenger side.

"Bye Mom," Will said to the driver, a middle-aged woman with a sharp, black bob, before closing the door and walking towards Vera with a bright smile.

"Still don't have your license?" Vera teased. "That sucks."

Will pretended to look hurt. "I think I need a hug for

that."

Vera laughed, but took a step forward and put her arms around Will. He was warm like always, and Vera was smiling when she stepped away.

"Better?" Vera asked. Will grinned, tugging on a bouncy copper curl, reminding Vera of Aspen like a sharp pain in her side that she tried to ignore.

"Much better," Will said. The sunshine that seemed to radiate off of him made Vera feel better.

They bought the tickets, popcorn, and drinks before finding their seat in Theater 2. It was dark, and Vera could just make out Will's white teeth almost glowing as he flashed her another smile. The trailers were already playing when they sat down.

Vera sipped on her soda. Will ate a large handful of popcorn. Then another.

"You're gonna finish that before the movie even starts," Vera whispered when he began grabbing another handful.

"The trailers are the best part," Will said.

"Shh!" someone said furiously behind them. Vera and Will turned to each other with wide eyes. Vera stifled giggles, and Will bit his lip to keep from laughing. Then the movie began.

Immediately the suspense grew, and Vera found herself

curled in her seat, gripping the bowl of popcorn. When Harry Styles appeared on the screen, Vera turned her head to comment, but Will must've had the same idea because Vera found her face a breath away from his.

Will's eyes widened. Vera swallowed uneasily. Neither of them pulled away. For a second, an image flickered in Vera's mind, of black hair and blue eyes, and she almost felt like she was cheating. It was a ridiculous thought, since absolutely nothing had happened between them. *And nothing ever will,* Vera reminded herself.

Will's eyes flickered down to her lips. If she kissed him, everything would change. They would no longer be friends, but something *more*. And anything *more* with Aspen would fade away, forever just a figment of her imagination.

She leaned in closer. Or maybe Will did. A bit further and everything would end. Why did she sound so morbid? What was wrong with her?

But she knew what was wrong. She didn't want to kiss Will.

Suddenly the sound of a huge explosion rocked the movie theater, startling Vera and Will away from each other. Vera's breath turned shallow, and she turned her eyes back to the screen so Will wouldn't see the relief that was surely reflected on her face.

6

Vera's alarm sounded at six o'clock sharp, blaring through the room in an attempt to wake her up. Not only did she wake up, but she also managed to knock her head back against the headboard of her bed, and she groaned.

After she dressed quickly, Vera hurried downstairs for breakfast, still rubbing her throbbing head. Layla was there, already eating, as well as her parents.

"Good morning," Layla chirped. Vera glared at her, not in the mood for any sunshine or smiles. Layla raised an eyebrow. "Someone woke up on the wrong side of the bed."

Their mom was sipping on her morning coffee, and their dad was reading the news on his iPad.

"So, what did you girls do yesterday?" their mom asked, glancing at both of them curiously. "Both of you came home after dinner."

Vera looked at Layla. Didn't she and Aspen hang out

at home?

"Aspen and I hung out at a friend's house, and then we went to the mall," Layla said.

"A boy's house?" their mom asked.

"He's gay," Layla said defensively.

"Are you sure he's gay?" It was their dad. He had put down his iPad, deciding to join the conversation. For some reason, Vera tensed at the subject.

"Like, ninety-nine percent sure," Layla said. Then she turned to Vera, hastily trying to turn the attention on her instead. "How about you, Vera? I saw you go out last night before we did."

Vera forced a casual smile. "I watched Dunkirk with a friend."

Layla narrowed her eyes but didn't comment. Their parents smiled at the thought of Vera socializing and going outside instead of reading in her room.

"I heard it was a very good movie," their dad said.

Vera nodded. It was an amazing movie, and it would have been spectacular if the incident with Will and all the following awkwardness hadn't occurred.

"We should go," Vera told Layla, and they quickly gathered their belongings.

Once the doors of the car closed, Layla raised a brow. "Which friend did you see Dunkirk with?"

Uh oh. If Layla was suspicious, that meant she might have seen either Piper or Jane at the mall.

"Why do you care?" Vera asked irritably. It must've been something in her tone that gave her away because Layla's face lit up.

"I knew it! You went to the movies with Will, didn't you," Layla said.

Vera sighed. There was no point in lying. "Yes, I did. And no, nothing happened. We are just friends. End of story."

"Well, you're no fun," Layla said, then plugged in her phone and turned up the music loud for the rest of the ride to school.

Piper reacted in a similar way when Vera told her nothing had happened. Even Jane looked a bit startled.

"So he didn't even try to hold your hand?" Jane asked.

"Again, nothing happened. I told you, we're just friends," Vera said. Jane shrugged, ready to move on, but Piper was still in shock.

"It didn't seem like you guys were 'just friends' yesterday. You were blushing and stuttering. And his beautiful smile. I mean, come *on!*" Piper exclaimed.

Vera frowned. She didn't tell them that yesterday she thought she did like Will, and that when they almost kissed, she realized that she didn't. Vera also didn't tell them about her conversation with Aspen, her sister's best friend who was definitely off limits, and how she felt when they held hands.

No, Vera didn't say any of that, but when she said, "Nothing happened," for the third time, Piper and Jane must've picked up on something in her tone, because for the rest of the day they never brought Will up again.

Vera pushed down her guilt at the thought of Will. She had ignored the tenth text from him to hang out, along with a few amusing gifs. While she was grateful that he was trying to act like nothing happened, Vera still didn't want to see him again so soon.

Her phone vibrated in her pocket, and she groaned, prepared to see another text from Will. But it was Layla.

Layla: Getting a ride from a dance friend. See you later.

When she got home, the house was silent, as it always was on Friday afternoons when her sister had dance class until dinner and her parents were working late. Vera, on the other hand, liked to read or catch up on her TV shows. She was about to pick up the book she was currently reading when her phone rang.

Vera nearly dropped her phone when she saw the name

on the screen.

Aspen.

"Hello?" Vera answered.

"Hey, Vera, do you…" Aspen paused. "Could I come over? To talk?"

"Is it about your father?" Vera asked, a bit panicked. What if something had happened? Vera wouldn't know what to do.

"No. He's fine. Something else," Aspen said. Vera's heart was already thumping loudly in her chest, almost painfully. "Is Layla there?"

"She's at dance class," Vera said. Before she changed her mind, she added, "So you can come over if you want."

Vera thought she heard a short intake of breath on the other end of the line before Aspen spoke.

"I'll be there in ten."

Aspen arrived ten minutes later in her signature red, today a pair of Converse high tops and a white mini dress with a pattern of small red roses.

"Hi," Vera said, hating how nervous she sounded.

"I like your shorts," Aspen said. Vera looked down, startled. She was wearing loose summer shorts, but Vera didn't think they were anything special.

"Do you want something to drink?" Vera asked, struggling to keep her voice from wavering.

"A glass of water, please," Aspen said quietly. They moved to the kitchen. Vera filled a glass with water, her hands trembling slightly. She handed the glass to Aspen. "Thank you."

Vera stood awkwardly as Aspen took a sip and brought the glass down, looking at Vera steadily.

"Why don't we go to your room?" Aspen asked. Vera's eyes widened, and she forced herself to look casual. She didn't even know why this surprised her. Hanging out in someone's room was completely normal.

"Sure," Vera said. So why did walking up the stairs with Aspen following silently make her blush?

When they entered Vera's room, she cringed, wishing she had cleaned the room a bit. Her school uniform was draped over her chair, her backpack was on the floor, and her closet doors were open, revealing her messily organized clothes. The only neat part of the room was her bed, as Vera had remembered to make it this morning.

Vera quickly walked over and shut the closet doors. Aspen was walking towards her bed. Why was Vera's heart racing like that? And how could she make it stop?

"Don't tell Layla," Aspen said, smoothing out the covers with a flat palm, "but I like your bed more than hers."

Vera swallowed, then sat on the bed, holding her breath when Aspen narrowly hid a smile and did the same, sitting beside her. Then Aspen scooted down so she was flat on her back, staring at the ceiling, and without thinking, Vera copied her movements, their arms brushing as she got settled on what now felt like a very small bed.

"What do you want to talk about?" Vera asked, her voice quiet.

Aspen shifted slightly and took in a deep breath. "I like someone. A lot. And I need your advice."

Vera deflated. That was what Aspen wanted to talk about?

"Is it someone at school?" Vera asked, trying to ignore the sick feeling curling in her stomach.

"Yes," Aspen whispered. Vera felt that sick feeling turn into jealousy, fast and hot in her blood, before she could stop it.

"And you couldn't talk to Layla about this?" Vera asked coldly. She regretted saying it the moment she did, but Vera still couldn't get rid of the churning nausea inside her, the burning behind her eyes. *Don't cry, Vera, about something as stupid as this.*

"No, I couldn't," Aspen replied, clearly ignoring her

icy tone. "Because you see, it's a girl."

The world stopped. Vera tried to think, to speak, but her body and mind had stopped functioning and her vision was hazy at the edges.

Aspen continued, "She's smart. Beautiful. And I don't know what to do."

Vera lay very still, the jealousy in her stomach sizzling into dread. This scenario hadn't even crossed her mind. She hadn't considered the possibility that if Aspen liked girls, she would already like someone else.

Beside her, Aspen turned towards Vera. Seemingly against her will, Vera turned too, until she was on her side, face to face with Aspen.

"I just…" Aspen's voice trailed off as her eyes darted down to Vera's mouth. And suddenly Vera realized, and her stomach flipped, and her whole body froze under those blue eyes. Aspen moved closer to Vera like they were two magnets drawn together. "I just want her so badly. Is that wrong?"

"No," Vera said, breathless. So this was *want*. She understood the difference now. Her heartbeat drummed in her ears, her fingertips, and there was a hook in her stomach, dragging her closer to the only thing that mattered in this moment. It was almost painful, every inch of her skin aching, her body yearning, as if it realized that the something that had been missing all along was this.

Vera's eyes fluttered closed. The seconds grew longer, her heartbeat slower, just before their lips brushed, hesitant, feather-like, from one breath to the next.

The door downstairs slammed open. "I'm home!"

Layla.

7

Aspen was off the bed in a blink of an eye, grabbing her purse and quietly walking out the door. Vera's chest tightened. *What was Aspen doing?*

Vera got up, legs shaking as she tiptoed to the door, straining her ears to listen. She didn't dare go outside.

Layla was already stomping up the stairs, so that meant Aspen hadn't gone downstairs. Maybe she was hiding in the bathroom. A door opened. Silence.

"Aspen!" Layla exclaimed. "What are you doing here?"

"I came to surprise you!" Aspen lied. It was so convincing that for a moment Vera thought that she had imagined everything.

"You're the best!" Layla said with a squeal, and then the door to her room closed and Vera could hear no more.

Vera walked back to her bed, sitting down on the edge. Her breaths were coming out too fast, and the knot in her chest wasn't loosening.

She went to the bathroom, studying her reflection in

the mirror. Her cheeks were red, and her eyes were dazed. Vera brought a hand up to her face, touching her lips with her fingertips. Her face felt hot, and she was winded, as if she had just finished a run.

Vera ran the cold water and splashed some on her face. A little better, but she still felt scattered, as if a ripping wind had torn through her body. With some determination, Vera went downstairs and grabbed her keys.

She didn't quite know where she was going, but her mind must've been set on something because she pulled into the familiar parking lot of her favorite used bookstore twenty minutes later.

It was an old bookstore, and between the brick walls, old-fashioned furniture, industrial lamps, and the small cafe in the back supplying outlets, one could see where old mixed with new. She liked to buy a book and read it in one of the cushy armchairs between aisles, or buy a coffee and do her homework at one of the tables.

Today Vera went straight to the New Fiction section, hoping to spend the money she earned at the fair. After all, there was nothing quite like the feeling of buying a book.

Her fingers ran along the spines, reading the titles. She smiled at the ones she had already read, pulling out the ones she had heard about, skimming the summaries.

After half an hour of searching through the rows of books, she narrowed her decision down to two books. One was a fantasy thriller, the other a teen fiction comedy. One had an unsure ending, and one was bound to end happily. One was the dangerous choice, the other safe.

Usually, Vera chose the safer one, but for some reason, she slid the teen fiction comedy back on the shelf, bringing the fantasy thriller to the checkout counter.

After paying, Vera took the book and settled in a chair. Once she started reading the book, allowing her mind to follow the words into another world, her shoulders relaxed, and her breathing settled into a shallow rhythm. She must've read for an hour or so when she noticed someone standing beside her chair. Vera looked up.

"Aspen?" Vera dropped the book, forgetting to put a bookmark, and stood up quickly, nearly knocking the chair to the ground. "How did you find me?"

Aspen smiled. "I remember a year ago your parents took us here to pick you up." She paused, smirking. "And I also stole Layla's phone to check Find My iPhone."

Vera laughed. "But what did you tell Layla?"

"I told her I actually had to go home because of my dad. Besides, Layla said she was meeting some guy." Aspen took a step forward, her blue eyes traveling over Vera's face.

"What are you doing here?" Vera asked. The breathing problem was coming back. How was Aspen so composed? Maybe because she's done this before, sneered a voice in her head. The thought popped up in Vera's mind before she could stop it. A second later, Aspen's gaze dropped lower and erased all thoughts from Vera's mind.

"You didn't think that I was going to leave it at that, did you?" Aspen asked, arching a brow.

Vera's heart stuttered. "What?"

Aspen laughed, then grinned. She gently grabbed Vera's wrist and walked them back through the main hall, turning behind the bookshelf marked Historical Fiction, and leading them to a dark corner.

"Let me know if you want to stop," Aspen whispered, before pulling Vera close.

8

Vera's heart beat loudly in her ears, and her face was on fire.

Every time Aspen's fingers pressed into her hips, it was like riding on a roller coaster just as it plummeted to the ground, when her breath flew out of her and her stomach dropped, and for a moment she was terrified that she would fall and nothing would catch her.

"Let's get out of here," Aspen said between kisses. Vera barely nodded before Aspen's wrist hooked behind Vera's neck and they were kissing again.

All Vera could think about was Aspen's mouth against hers, soft and gentle and faintly sweet. But the most shocking thing was not just kissing Aspen. It was the effect she had on her, on this beautiful *girl*. Whenever Vera placed a light hand on Aspen's waist, she shivered. It was a shock. It was a dream. Vera's head was light.

"I just can't stop," Aspen said, breaking away and trying to catch her breath. Vera's skin sparked where Aspen's fingers circled her wrists, keeping her only a foot away. Aspen's cheeks were flushed, and her eyes bright.

"We can drive somewhere," Vera said, then blushed at her words. She hardly knew what they meant. Aspen smiled, then pulled Vera close and pressed a chaste kiss on her lips. Then she dragged Vera out to the main hall, Vera hardly remembered to pick her book up on the way out.

"Where do you want to go?" Vera asked, starting the car.

"How about my place?" Aspen suggested. An image of Vera on Aspen's bed, their arms wrapped around each other, flashed across her mind.

Vera glanced at Aspen, who had a small smile dancing on her lips, and she blushed again.

"Oh, my mom's calling," Aspen said, looking at her phone. She answered. "Hey Mom, what's up?"

Suddenly Aspen sucked in a breath.

"What? Oh my god. I'll be there right away. Okay, yes, bye." Aspen put down her phone and turned to Vera with wide, panicked eyes. "My dad's been admitted to the hospital."

A tear fell down Aspen's cheek, and she wiped at it hastily with the back of her hand. Vera felt a slight panic rise in her chest, but she pushed it down. One of them had to be in control, and it wasn't going to be Aspen.

"Which hospital?" Vera asked.

Aspen stifled a sob, breathing unevenly. "West Valley Hospital Center."

Vera knew where it was. She had gone to West Valley Hospital when she broke her arm in third grade. It was right across from a large Target building and a Barnes & Noble, and once she had been well enough to be released, her mom had taken her to buy a few books.

With her heart in her throat, Vera merged back into traffic and drove as fast as she could.

The drive was forty-five minutes because it was rush-hour traffic. Vera honked at any car that was remotely slow and weaved through traffic to the best of her ability. Aspen was crying silently the whole time, her face stunned. All Vera could do was tell her that they would be there soon.

Vera had never felt so helpless before.

"Okay, I'll drop you off in front, then I'll find parking," Vera said.

Aspen nodded with a shuddering breath. When they pulled up in front of the hospital, Aspen jumped out and rushed towards the doors. Vera could just make out Aspen's frantic mother behind the sliding glass doors before driving away to find a parking spot.

By the time Vera parked and entered the hospital, Aspen and her mother were sitting on waiting chairs, Aspen's head resting on her mother's shoulder.

Vera stopped short. She was about to go sit with them when it suddenly occurred to her that she should not be there at all. Vera nearly turned around before they spotted her when Aspen called her name.

"Vera! Wait!"

Vera turned to see Aspen walking towards her, eyes still red from crying. When she reached Vera, Aspen hugged her, and Vera was immediately engulfed in her sweet perfume.

"Thank you so much for driving me."

It took Vera a few moments to realize she was not hugging her back, and hesitantly wrapped her arms around Aspen. "You're welcome." And before she could protest, Aspen was pulling her toward her mother, who looked at Vera in surprise. "Aspen, wait—"

"Vera, this is my mom. Mom, this is Vera," Aspen said. "I don't think you guys have been properly introduced. Vera drove me here."

"Nice to meet you, Mrs. Silva," Vera said automatically.

Her mom raised a brow, slightly confused. "Nice to meet you too. Correct me if I am wrong, Vera, but are you not Layla's sister?"

Vera smiled forcibly. "Yes, I am."

Aspen sat beside her mom, dragging Vera down to the seat next to her. Vera scooted slightly away from Aspen, feeling Mrs. Silva's eyes on her.

"Where is Layla?" Her mom asked, turning to Aspen. "She didn't want to come?"

Vera's pulse quickened in fear, and Aspen tensed next to her.

"Well, I was at Layla's and she had dance practice. Vera offered to drive me home after dropping off Layla, and then you called."

Her mom nodded, then smiled. "Thank you, Vera. That was very nice of you."

Vera's insides twisted. She hated lying to well-meaning adults. It always made her feel like she had already done something wrong before getting in trouble.

"Mrs. Silva?"

All three of them looked up. A man in blue scrubs holding a clipboard had stepped into the waiting room and was looking around. Mrs. Silva and Aspen shot up. Vera was about to stand up with them when she remembered that only family would be allowed to visit.

Vera settled back in her cushioned chair as Aspen and her mom disappeared through the sliding doors. Her eyelids felt heavy, and her body drained, as the day's events began to catch up with her.

Perhaps she could rest her eyes for a few minutes. No one would kick her out of the waiting room. Before she could change her mind, Vera closed her eyes, and the world faded to black as she fell asleep.

9

"Vera."

Someone shook her shoulders gently. Vera opened her eyes sleepily, and winced at the blinding fluorescent lights. Aspen was standing above her, a hand on Vera's shoulder. That touch alone sent a flutter through Vera's stomach.

"Aspen, hey," Vera said, her voice hoarse. She yawned, stretching her back and neck, which were stiff from sleeping in an awkward position.

"You stayed?" Aspen asked.

Vera nodded, embarrassed. She glanced around the waiting room, then saw that it was dark outside. "What time is it?"

"Almost 1 a.m."

Vera sat up straight, pulling out her phone. Sure enough, there were missed calls from her parents, texts from Layla, and also from Will. She knew she could come up with a good excuse for her parents, but Layla had a way of knowing when she was lying.

Layla: Where are you?

Layla: Mom and dad are mad. Can you at least answer them?

Vera put her phone away, not even bothering to read the other texts. She would deal with them later.

"I'm going to stay here with my mom," Aspen said with a sad smile. "You should go home."

"Are you sure?"

Aspen nodded, glancing away awkwardly. "Before Layla gets suspicious."

Hearing her sister's name startled Vera back into reality. Aspen was right. She had to go home.

"Okay, I'll go," Vera relented. "But you're okay? Or, as okay as you can be?"

Aspen smiled, though it didn't reach her eyes. "I'm okay. Now go."

Soon enough Vera was pulling into her driveway, the car ride home having passed in lingering shock at the dream-like day which was slowly coming to an end. She could hardly believe it was only that afternoon she kissed Aspen on her bed.

Inside, Layla was sitting on the couch on the phone with one of her friends. When she saw Vera, Layla said a quick goodbye and hung up.

"Where were you?" Layla asked.

Vera shrugged. "Piper's house. We were watching a movie. Started it too late." She hated how easily the lies left her mouth. Layla looked like she half-believed her, which was all Vera needed.

"Well, Mom and Dad were upset that you missed dinner and didn't even say anything," Layla muttered, returning to her phone. Vera took this as her cue to leave.

"I'll just talk to them in the morning," Vera said as she walked up the stairs.

In her room, she heard Layla resume her quiet phone call. Vera crawled under the covers of her bed with a grateful sigh, and nearly forgot to take off her glasses as she fell swiftly asleep.

Vera's door slammed open.

"Vera! Wake up now!"

Vera groaned, slamming a pillow over her head to block out her sister's loud voice. The pillow was snatched from her hands. "Hey!"

"Aspen just called me."

Vera froze, then sat up. Did she tell Layla everything?

But Layla did not look angry, only worried. "And?" Vera was surprised her voice didn't waver.

Layla was standing next to her bed, arms crossed. "And her dad is in the hospital! Aspen's at home now and I need you to drive me there. It's serious."

Vera forced her eyes to widen in surprise. This was more difficult than she thought it would be. "Oh wow. Okay, I'll get ready."

Layla narrowed her eyes. "Hurry up." Then she left the room.

Vera let out a sigh just as her phone vibrated on her nightstand. She picked it up. Another text from Will. Vera cringed and ignored his text. She still couldn't think about him without feeling embarrassed.

After getting dressed quickly, Vera found Layla eating cereal downstairs, holding a bouquet in her hand. Vera took a bowl of cereal for herself, though her appetite was rapidly shrinking the more she thought of seeing Aspen. What if Aspen regretted kissing her? What if Layla found out? Oh god, and Vera looked awful! She was wearing sweatpants and her hair was not even brushed.

Vera almost considered going upstairs to change when her sister ushered them out of the house and all too soon they were walking up to Aspen's front door, Vera awkwardly holding the bouquet. Vera tried to calm her nerves with deep breaths, but after one odd glance from Layla, she gave up the effort.

Layla rang the doorbell.

A few moments later they heard footsteps and the door swung open. Aspen was standing on the other side. Her face lit up at the sight of her best friend, and when her gaze landed on Vera and the bouquet, Aspen's eyes widened.

"I brought you these" Layla said, taking the flowers from Vera and handing them to Aspen.

"Thank you," Aspen said, her gaze flickering to Vera before smiling.

"Can I come in?" Layla asked.

"Of course." Aspen stepped back and Layla walked inside. Vera hung back, since she had to drive back home. "Are you not coming in too?"

Vera went still and looked at Layla, who shrugged. "I don't mind."

Aspen gestured for her to come in, and Vera could not resist. She followed them into the living room. Vera met Aspen's eyes and blushed, looking away. Maybe she should have left when she had the chance.

Layla sat on the couch, Aspen taking a seat beside her. Vera sat down in the armchair next to them. There was an awkward pause.

"So…how's your dad doing?" Layla asked hesitantly. Vera turned to glare at Layla for bringing up the sensitive subject, but Aspen was smiling brightly.

"He's actually doing great! Last night was a bit of a scare, but he's going to be alright."

Layla clapped her hands together. "That's amazing Aspen!"

Vera sighed in relief. She hadn't realized how anxious she had been about Aspen's father until now.

"So…" Layla's smile morphed into a mischievous grin that Vera knew all too well. "How are you and Maxwell doing?"

Aspen's eyes widened, and Vera's stomach dropped.

She couldn't hold back the question. "Is Maxwell your boyfriend?" There was that dread again, curling in her stomach. It was easy to forget about boys and high school drama when Vera was kissing Aspen alone. But with Layla here, everything was brought into perspective.

"No, he's not," Aspen said at the same time as Layla said, "Basically."

Layla looked at Aspen, confused. "No? I thought…"

"I don't like him," Aspen said decidedly. "He's not really my type."

"Oh?" Layla was staring at Aspen as if she was a stranger. "I didn't know you had a type."

"Oh I definitely have a type," Aspen said tersely, and Vera felt her face grow hot.

Layla raised a brow at the tone, but held back what surely was a biting response. They had just recently made up, and besides, Aspen's dad had been in the hospital.

"Do you want to watch a movie?" Layla asked abruptly, changing the subject.

Aspen glanced at Vera, but her face was hard to read. "Sure. We can watch it on my TV in my room if you want."

"I think I'll go home," Vera said, standing up. Aspen and Layla both looked at her startled, as if they had forgotten she was there. "But can I use your bathroom first?"

Aspen shot up. "I'll show you where it is."

Layla stood up and started walking upstairs. "I'll set it up. See you later, Vera."

Aspen led Vera down the hall and around a corner before she suddenly turned towards Vera and took her face in her hands, her eyes wide and blue. "*You're* my type." And then they were kissing.

Vera was so surprised that by the time she realized what was happening, Aspen was already walking back to the living room.

10

Vera decided to meet with Will today. It was Sunday, and all she had to do was homework. If she didn't talk with Will today, she would have to tiptoe around him for the rest of the week.

They were planning to meet at the park next to a local field where Will's lacrosse team practiced. He finished practice at 3 p.m., so if the conversation didn't go well, she planned to go on a run around the park.

"Are you okay?" Layla asked, looking over her phone at Vera. They were sitting together on the couch, Vera attempting to read her assigned book and Layla re-watching the Titanic on the TV. "You look like you're going to throw up. It's not the movie, is it?"

"I'm just nervous," Vera said. She put her book down. It was useless. The words were nearly blurring together on the pages.

Layla looked at Vera curiously. "Why? Meeting someone?"

"Yeah. Will. From the fair."

Layla tensed, then averted her eyes. "Do you like him?" she asked distractedly, already looking on her phone again.

"No, I don't," Vera replied firmly, hoping Layla wouldn't question her about it.

"Oh, okay." Vera thought Layla sounded relieved.

Vera checked her phone and realized it was a quarter to three. "I should go." Then she got up and left before Layla could respond.

Will was already waiting next to the field, a bit sweaty, and still in some of his lacrosse gear which was dirtied from mud and grass. Vera walked to him reluctantly, her heart beating quickly. When he saw her, Will smiled, but it didn't reach his eyes.

"Hey," Will said.

Vera waved. "Hey."

They stared at each other for a few seconds before Vera blurted out, "I have to tell you something!" at the same time as Will said, "I have a confession to make—"

They laughed nervously.

Will scratched the back of his neck. "You first."

"No, you first," Vera said, raising a brow.

"At the same time then," Will offered.

Vera paused. Was she really going to do this? What if

Will was about to admit that he was in love with her or something? *No.* She couldn't back out now. Will deserved to know.

"Okay. On the count of three," Vera said. "One, two ….three!"

"Your sister and I kissed!" Will said at the same time as Vera said, "I like girls!"

They both stared at each other, shocked into silence.

"Wow," Will said after a long silence.

"Wow," Vera repeated, a little dazed. She really had not seen that coming. For a second, she was thrilled, because this solved everything. But then she remembered that Layla had a boyfriend. Though this did explain Layla's annoyance earlier when Vera had said she was going to meet up with Will.

"So…you like girls?" Will asked.

"So…you like my sister?" Vera asked, ignoring the heat blooming on her cheeks. She searched Will's face, trying to find the dreaded disgust or anger or disappointment. But there was nothing besides a mild mixture of surprise, curiosity, and a little fear, probably due to her question.

No one spoke. Neither of them knew where to go from here, and both of them were too stubborn to be the first on the hot seat. But as the seconds ticked by, Vera felt her stomach roll anxiously, and she couldn't wait any longer.

"So you're not…angry?" Vera asked hesitantly.

Will's brows furrowed, and if Vera wasn't mistaken, he looked almost offended. "Vera…of course I'm not angry. I realize I never told you, but I have two moms." He smiled warmly. "I'm adopted!"

Vera's mouth fell open, and she laughed nervously. That's why Will's mom in the car looked nothing like him. "That's amazing! I had no idea."

"Well, you can meet them one day if you want," Will said. "They've heard a lot about you."

"That would be lovely!" Vera was so happy at the turn of events that she nearly forgot about Will's confession. "Wait. You need to explain how you and Layla happened."

Will sighed, looking down at his feet which scuffed the ground. "It was a few days ago, when you weren't answering my calls or texts. I was walking near your house, thinking I might run into you. But instead I saw Layla, who was taking a walk. She told me that you were not home, but offered to hang out, and I said yes. We started talking about you, and then about Aspen, and how she felt that both of you were ignoring her. I don't know how it happened. As I was leaving, she started tearing up and I tried to console her and then we kissed."

"I thought she had a boyfriend?" Vera asked slowly.

"Yeah," Will said, his eyes darkening. "Still does. And she really likes him too. After we kissed, she sort of freaked out and I left. Haven't talked to her since."

He looked a little saddened by it. Vera didn't know what to say. It had always seemed to her that Layla really liked the guy she was dating. She just couldn't imagine her sister and Will kissing. It reminded her of Dunkirk and their almost-kiss. What would her life be like, if she had leaned in and kissed him? Would she be happy, or even more miserable?

"Did you…did you ever like me?" Vera asked.

Will shrugged. "I think I did a little. But at the same time, I think a part of me knew we weren't meant to be together, you know?"

Vera nodded, breathing a sigh of relief. She had been afraid that Will would hold a grudge against her. "So we're still friends?"

"You can't get rid of me that easily," Will joked, playfully shoving Vera's shoulder. Suddenly he frowned. "Wait, I'm just curious. How did you realize you liked girls? Or did you always know?"

Vera hesitated. A part of her still didn't want to tell anyone, to keep this perfectly secret life to herself. But the other part, the part that desperately needed some advice, someone to share her fears and concerns, won out. "You can't tell anyone, okay? Especially not my sister," Vera warned.

Will's eyes widened at her tone. "Promise."

"Okay, then. It started one night when Aspen showed up drunk at my house…" Vera told him about the dress, the lace, the awkwardness of it all. She recalled the almost kiss on her bed, interrupted by Layla, and then kissing at the bookstore. Then she narrated the hospital incident and the weird interaction with Layla talking about a guy named Maxwell, and finally, the kiss down the hall.

She told the story in nearly one breath, and at the end of it, Will's face was stunned. Vera slapped him lightly on the arm, and he straightened up with a sheepish smile.

"Sorry, I'm just super shocked right now. *Aspen?* As in your sister's *best friend?*" Will shook his head. "I mean, I heard the rumors about Aspen cheating on her boyfriend with a girl, but I didn't think it was actually true."

"That wasn't me," Vera said. "That was the night she came to my house drunk. And she told me a day or so after that she got drunk because her boyfriend broke up with her because she kissed…she kissed…" Realization dawned on Vera. "I don't think she ever told me who she kissed."

Will whistled. "Who cares about that? I still can't believe you and Aspen kissed. She doesn't exactly strike me as your type."

Vera rolled her eyes at Will's smirk. "Let me guess, you're my type?"

"I'm everybody's type," Will said, frowning. "But seriously, you and Aspen?"

"I didn't think I was her type either," Vera admitted, then added thoughtfully, "in more ways than one."

Will laughed. "This day keeps getting stranger and stranger. First, you like girls. Then Aspen likes you. And now you're actually funny! Unbelievable."

Vera crossed her arms as Will continued to laugh at his own joke. "You're acting very calm for a boy who just kissed my sister."

Will threw his hands up. "Okay, okay! I'm sorry. But it *is* funny. Your sister's *best friend!*"

"Don't make me regret telling you," Vera said, but even she felt herself beginning to smile.

11

Aspen hadn't texted, called, or spoken to her since Saturday. Now it was Monday, and although she and Will had cleared the air, Vera still felt distracted and anxious in all her classes. Piper and Jane didn't mention anything, but Vera knew they had picked up on her vacant stares and long silences.

But how was she supposed to tell them about Aspen if she herself didn't even know what was going on between them? Vera supposed *she* could reach out to Aspen, but the thought of giving in so easily made her hesitate.

After all, Vera couldn't forget what she learned about Aspen. If Aspen could cheat on her boyfriend, what's going to stop her from cheating on Vera? And that was assuming Vera and Aspen were dating, which only made the matter worse.

Because Aspen was…well, Aspen. And Vera was nothing special, without considering that she was Aspen's best friend's *sister*. In Vera's eyes, she was undesirable on multiple levels. Perhaps the best thing to do was back out while she still had the chance.

When Vera returned home from school, she was immediately greeted by the smell of something delicious cooking in the kitchen. Her mom's head popped out from behind the open fridge.

"Hey sweetie," her mom said with a smile. "How was school?"

And just like that, another wave of reality came crashing down. Vera had completely forgotten that she would have to tell her parents about liking girls. Or rather, she had completely ignored that fact. She forced a smile now, hoping she did not look as awful as she felt.

"It was good," Vera said, inching towards the stairs.

Her mom rolled her eyes. "Always the same answer every day. At least tell me something new today."

Vera paused on the first step of the staircase. She could easily tell her about Aspen, and just get it over with. Vera took a step down and walked over to the kitchen before she lost her nerve.

"I actually need some advice," Vera said slowly.

Her mother frowned. "Oh? On what?"

"Well, you see…" Vera bit her lip. *I really like Layla's best friend, Aspen, and we kissed and I don't know what to do without ruining both relationships. What do you think I should do?* "…there's a girl at school who I'm sort of friends with, and she told me that she's bisexual. What should I do?"

Her mom stared at her blankly for a moment, before laughing. "Oh sweetie, what's there to worry about? Okay, so she's bisexual. That doesn't mean she's going to kiss you. That's just who she is. Tell her that being bisexual doesn't make you look at her any differently. Then move on."

Vera blinked. It had not been the reaction she had expected. "Really?"

Her mom laughed, reaching over to tuck a loose strand of Vera's hair behind her ear with an affectionate smile. "Sometimes I forget how sheltered you both are."

"I'm not sheltered!" Vera protested, but she was smiling, because even though her mom didn't know it, she had erased some of the fear Vera had of telling her.

Then Vera felt her phone buzz. She looked at the screen and saw Aspen's name glaring at her in small print, right above a new text message.

Aspen: We should talk.

Vera's fingers hovered over the screen. A part of her was relieved that Aspen had finally texted her back, but the other part of her sensed that something was about to change, and she wasn't sure she was ready for it.

Vera: How about tomorrow after school?

Aspen: My house okay?

Vera: Yes, see you then.

Vera went upstairs and collapsed onto her bed. How had her life become this complicated this quickly? Only a few weeks ago her biggest worry was a math test, and now it was about her relationship with her sister's best friend and coming out to her parents.

How could she not have realized that she liked girls?

Vera tried to remember ever liking a girl like she liked Aspen. Slowly, she began to recollect a few moments of her imagination running a little too wild, a few dreams whose memories caused her to blush. Vera used to think it was natural. Just mere curiosity.

But now when she thought of kissing a boy, it started to feel uncomfortable as she tried to imagine doing anything more than just kissing. Then she thought of Aspen, on her bed, a hand sliding underneath her shirt…Vera blushed at how appealing that was to her.

Maybe Vera hadn't acknowledged these fantasies because, before this past month, she had no real experience with either boys or girls. Except for that one boy in sophomore year from her Math class, and did that really even count? Vera hadn't liked him at all, and the kiss was inexperienced and sloppy.

Suddenly there was a knock on the door.

"Come in!"

The door opened hesitantly before Layla walked in. "Hey," she said quietly. "I just wanted to talk."

For a split second, Vera thought that maybe Will had told Layla everything. But that was irrational. Will was a nice person, and would never do that to Vera.

Still, Vera's heart pounded in her chest. "About what?"

Layla bit her lip. "What's going on with you lately?"

Vera froze. There were a million things she could say, but the one she *should* say wasn't what she felt like talking about at the moment.

"Just stressed about college applications," Vera said, which was mostly true. But she had already sent in all her applications, and now she just had to wait.

"Oh. Well, you're so smart, you don't have to worry," Layla said.

Vera smiled. "Thanks." Then after a beat of silence, "If that's all…"

"No!" Layla blurted out, then grimaced. "I have something to tell you. Actually."

Suddenly the whole world seemed to slow down, and for some reason, Vera dreaded what Layla was going to say, even though she already had a good idea what it was.

"Go on," Vera encouraged.

Layla glanced around the room, tormented. Finally,

she sat down on the edge of her bed with a sigh. "I kissed Will," she said, then covered her face with a groan.

Vera felt guilt blossom in her stomach. *It's different with you,* a little voice whispered in Vera's mind. *She doesn't have to simultaneously come out.* Okay, fair point. But that guilt didn't fade.

"I know," Vera said.

Layla's hands left her face, her mouth parted in shock. "B-but how?"

"Will told me."

"Are you mad?" Layla asked fearfully.

Vera hesitated. "No…but don't you have a boyfriend?"

Layla's face crumbled, and Vera regretted bringing it up. Clearly this was a touchy subject.

"I mean, we have a thing right now, and he did ask if I wanted to date, and I said not yet. And I don't even know what happened with Will, like one moment we were just hanging out and the next we were kissing and it just felt right," Layla rambled, all in one breath. She stared at Vera helplessly.

"Look. Who do you like more?" Vera asked. "That's the guy you choose. Just don't keep Will around until you make that decision."

Layla nodded, and her eyes shone with the telltale sign of tears.

Vera sighed and opened her arms. "It's alright. Come here."

Layla cried as she collapsed into her arms. "I-I'm sorry," she hiccuped. "I'm a horrible person."

Vera stroked her back soothingly. "Of course not. Relationships are always complicated."

Layla's sobs slowed to quiet, shaking breaths. "You're the best sister ever," Layla mumbled.

This time the guilt struck her heart like a dagger, and it took all of her not to confess right then and there. "I love you," Vera said softly.

Layla relaxed in her arms. "Me too."

12

Vera lifted her hand to knock, then stopped. She took a deep breath. Why was she so scared? Maybe she knew deep down that this was the end of whatever brief moment they had together, and she was simply trying to delay the inevitable. Or maybe, just maybe, she was scared of what they could be, and the consequences they would then both have to face.

Suddenly the door swung open. Aspen stood on the other side, brow raised. "Hey."

"Hey," Vera said, barely a whisper. "I was just going to knock."

Aspen only shook her head fondly. "Come in."

She walked inside hesitantly, following after Aspen. Once inside, they both lingered on the landing, looking at the floor as if it were the most interesting thing in the house.

Then Aspen spoke first. "Want to go to my room?"

Vera thought it was probably not the best idea, but her

traitorous mouth decided for her. "Sure."

Aspen turned and led them upstairs, hands casually tucked into the pockets of her gray sweatpants. It was the first time Vera had seen her in such a casual outfit, with a plain white shirt instead of a crop top.

When they entered her room, Aspen's casual outfit suddenly seemed more intimate than it should. Vera didn't understand how Aspen was so well-composed. She herself blushed from head to toe, her heart beating wildly in her chest.

Aspen climbed on her bed, unbothered by the pink duvet draped carelessly over her mattress. She patted the bed next to her and frowned when Vera hesitated. "I think we're a little past that, don't you think?"

Vera blushed and sat down on the bed across from Aspen, who studied Vera's face for a moment before speaking.

"So I'm guessing you want a few explanations, right? About Kyle, and Maxwell?" Aspen asked, her voice un-wavering, almost cold. Vera realized it was a form of protection, not confidence.

"I just want honesty," Vera said softly.

Aspen bit her lip, glancing away. "You probably heard rumors about how Kyle and I broke up." Vera nodded. "Well, they were true. I was super drunk, and Kyle had pissed me off or something, and suddenly there was this pretty, openly bisexual girl in front of me, and we kissed. Kyle saw, and he broke up with me. That's it."

"Did you like Kyle?" Vera asked. Aspen shrugged.

"I liked kissing him. But I started wanting to kiss girls too, and then I knew I couldn't be with Kyle anymore until I figured myself out. I didn't think we would end that way though," Aspen said.

"How about the girl you kissed? Do you still like her?" Vera asked.

Aspen laughed and shook her head. "Sydney? No. I think we were both just sick of boys that night. It just happened."

Vera blanked, then nearly gasped. "Wait, Sydney? Like Sydney and Jack who just broke up because she cheated on—oh. This is making way more sense now."

Aspen giggled, and Vera shot her a halfhearted glare. "I promise you, she means nothing," Aspen said, turning serious. "We're not even really friends."

At this Vera relaxed a bit, now that the Kyle and Sydney situation was explained. But that still left the question of Maxwell.

"So who's Maxwell?" Vera asked. She braced herself for the worst possible answer, but Aspen just rolled her eyes.

"Maxwell is nothing," Aspen said, but catching Vera's

look, added, "He was some random guy who wanted to hook up with me. But I made it very clear that I wasn't interested."

"Why?" Vera asked without thinking.

"Because I don't like him," Aspen said simply.

"Why not just hook up with him so that no one thinks…so that you aren't suspicious?" Vera asked, and her face grew very hot.

Aspen looked at her curiously. "So that no one thinks what?"

Vera struggled to get the words out. "So that no one thinks you like girls, I guess." After all, it would be so easy. Who could suspect a girl like Aspen?

"But I don't care if people know," Aspen said.

"How can you not? Don't you care what people think?" Vera asked in disbelief.

"Fuck them," Aspen said, smirking. "Look. My philosophy is this: I like boys, I like girls, so what? It's nobody's business. If someone asks, then I'll tell them, and I'm not ashamed of it. I mean, I thought kissing Sydney would make it obvious, but apparently not."

Vera sat silent for a moment, then, "What about Layla?"

Aspen flinched at the name. She looked down, slightly ashamed. "That's different."

"Because her opinion actually matters to you?" Vera

asked. Aspen nodded and was silent. "Would you be willing to come out to her…with me?"

Aspen looked up at Vera sharply. "Yes."

"Really?"

"I like you, Vera. A lot, in case you didn't notice. You just make me crazy and I lose all control when I'm with you," Aspen said all at once, as if she had been meaning to tell Vera that for a long time.

"What about…what about boys?" Vera asked. She couldn't help herself.

Aspen smirked, leaning closer to Vera until their lips were a breath apart. "Well, boys…they're just missing some things, you know?"

"What things?" Vera asked, holding her breath as Aspen laid a gentle hand on her thigh.

"Well, they don't have your wavy brown hair," Aspen said, her hand traveling to Vera's hair and curling a strand around her finger. "They don't have your green eyes." Aspen pressed a light kiss on her cheek. "They don't have your full lips." She brushed her lips against Vera's, who swore her heartbeat was *everywhere.* Then Aspen's hand on her thigh inched forward. "And they don't have *this.*" Her eyes glanced down meaningfully as her finger brushed the front zipper of her jeans.

Vera's eyes widened, panic seizing her chest. "I-I

haven't…"

How could Aspen be so confident? Vera regretted not kissing Will, if only to feel more comfortable now. She should have kissed more people. She should have practiced. Vera almost laughed out loud. Who would she have practiced with anyway? Her pillow?

Aspen backed away, her hands moving into her lap. It wasn't like Vera didn't want Aspen to…to touch her, but at the same time she was completely out of her depth, and Aspen had the upper hand in everything. She didn't know what to say.

"I'm sorry," Aspen said. "I'm going way too fast. It's just…I guess I'm used to guys wanting me to cut to the chase. I forgot it must be different with girls."

Vera felt embarrassed. She was the older one here and yet she was more innocent and naive. "No—I mean—yes. Sorry." Vera took a steadying breath. "Don't feel bad, or apologize. I just don't have that much experience, so all of this is really new to me. Like not even the girl part. Just the kissing part."

"You mean, I was your first kiss?" Aspen asked incredulously.

"Oh, well, no." Vera shook her head. "It was some guy in sophomore year. I didn't like him at all, and it sucked. And it was once." Aspen nodded. Vera picked at a loose thread from the covers, wishing she could disappear from Aspen's careful eyes on her.

"So you haven't hooked up with other guys after that?" Aspen asked, sounding doubtful.

Another wave of embarrassment washed over Vera again. "No, I haven't. I guess I know why now."

Aspen shook her head in disbelief. "But—you're so beautiful! A-and smart, and nice, and thoughtful, and kind…How has no guy made a move on you since sophomore year?"

Vera stared at her, unable to speak. It was still a shock to hear Aspen talk about her like that. Aspen was looking at her so earnestly that it was hard to look away.

"I don't…"

"Vera?" Aspen asked, softly.

"Yeah?" Vera's voice came out like a breath.

"I like you for who you are. Everything. Your past experiences, your plans for the future, your morals and ideals. And if a person can't appreciate everything about you like I do, then it's their loss."

Vera reached out and took one of Aspen's hands, their fingers lacing together. She couldn't hide her blush, but for the first time, she didn't care. "You know, you're pretty incredible."

Aspen blushed, looking down at their joined hands.

"You bring out the best in me," she admitted.

"I don't think you give yourself enough credit," Vera said, frowning.

"I'm a mess, Vera. I party too much, and the entire Hilltop population thinks I've slept with every boy at school, which might as well be true. But with you…I'm none of that." Aspen squeezed her hand. "And when it comes to experience, just remember that this is my first time with a girl too, and I have no idea what I'm doing either."

Aspen's eyes shined with a vulnerability that Vera hadn't seen before. Vera inched closer until their lips brushed, and they were sharing the same air. Aspen skimmed a hand along the side of Vera's hip, and that touch alone sent shivers down her spine.

"We don't have to do anything yet if you don't want to," Aspen said quietly.

Vera reached out and settled her hand safely on Aspen's knee. "I want to."

Then Vera gently pressed her lips against Aspen's. The kiss was slow, gentle, Aspen's mouth opening ever so slightly, her lips warm and soft under Vera's. She gripped Aspen's knee tightly when Aspen tilted her head and parted her lips more.

Aspen pulled back, her eyes questioning. "Was that

okay?"

Vera nodded, her head still spinning from the kiss. She wanted to say, *It was more than okay. It was everything. It was lovely.* But instead, she nodded again, smiling.

Aspen gingerly tucked a strand of Vera's hair behind her ear, then leaned over and placed a soft kiss on her bare neck. Vera's eyes fluttered shut. Another kiss on her shoulder. On her collarbone. Vera realized she was holding her breath, and that her hands had subconsciously settled on either side of Aspen's waist, gradually pulling her closer.

But when Aspen sat back to take off her shirt, Vera touched her wrist, stopping her. Aspen looked embarrassed. "You don't want me to?"

"No, that's not…" Vera sighed. "I just…I'm not used to this. Doing this. And it's not that I don't like it. It's actually the opposite. I love it. Maybe too much. But I don't want to…go any further without knowing what this is, or what might come of it. Because if this is a one-time thing for you—"

"Of course not!" Aspen interrupted. "This is not a one-time thing for me. At all." She shook her head, half-smiling. "But if you're asking whether I want to be your girlfriend, then it's a yes."

Vera thought she heard wrong, though she was already

blushing. "What?"

"I want to be your girlfriend," Aspen repeated slowly, grinning, then her eyes widened. "Unless it's too soon? I mean, I would totally understand—"

"No!" Vera could not stop blushing now, and they both laughed nervously. "No. It's not too soon. But…we haven't even been on a date yet. How do you know you want to date me?"

Aspen smiled. "I think I've known for a while now. But we should go on a date soon to make it official."

"I think I've known for a while too," Vera said, surprised at her honesty, her body relaxing with a sigh of relief. Before she could lose her nerve, Vera leaned in and kissed Aspen, who went still in surprise, before wrapping her arms around Vera's waist and bringing their bodies closer than ever before.

Vera pressed her hands against the indents of Aspen's waist, then hesitantly slipped a hand under her shirt, touching hot, bare skin, and she felt Aspen's breath catch.

Aspen leaned back, her black hair tumbling over her shoulders. She lifted her shirt over her head, casting it aside as if it were only in the way. Vera's gaze wandered over Aspen's face, the dark blue eyes, down the tender muscles of her neck, the shallow dip between her collarbone where Vera suddenly, desperately wanted to kiss.

Then Vera's heart stopped.

Aspen was wearing a red lace bra, the same set from that fateful night.

"Do you like it?" Aspen asked, almost worriedly.

Instead of replying, Vera leaned close and grazed her fingertips along the hem of the delicate material. Aspen held her breath as Vera hooked a finger under the right strap, then lightly letting it snap back into place.

"Red's your color," Vera said quietly.

Aspen's hands trembled as she found the waistline of her sweatpants and tugged them off, revealing the same red lace underneath.

Vera's heart raced as she ran her hand across the lace at Aspen's hip. She brought a hand against Aspen's cheek, then closed the distance between them, finding herself addicted to that moment when their lips first touched. *She almost tastes like cherries,* Vera thought randomly.

It was clear that Aspen had more experience than her. Soon Aspen had her hands tangled in Vera's hair, tugging and pulling her closer at the same time so that Vera felt faint. She thought they would kiss forever.

Aspen broke away to bring her mouth down Vera's neck, kissing the soft, sensitive skin beneath her jaw, on the curve of her shoulder. Vera pulled away before she would get carried away.

"Hold on," Vera said. Aspen sat upright, wondering. "I don't have lace like you. So don't expect anything special."

Aspen's eyes widened when she understood. A hint of a smile appeared on Vera's face, but she quickly dropped it when she saw the intensity of Aspen's gaze. Vera lifted the shirt up and cast it on the floor. Then without thinking Vera slipped out of her jeans.

She was only wearing a black bralette and plain cotton underwear, but Aspen looked at her with flushed cheeks and lowered eyelids.

Feeling emboldened by this reaction, Vera slid close and said, "You know, one day we should go shopping for some lace."

Aspen raised a brow, then lowered her head to find Vera's mouth with hers. They kissed tenderly, more deeply now, as Aspen cupped the back of Vera's neck to bring her closer.

In between kisses, Aspen joked, "Maybe that should be our first date."

Vera laughed, then pulled her in for another kiss.

13

Everything about Thursday was an accident.

Vera had accidentally left her lip balm at Aspen's house the day before. It must've fallen out of her pocket. Instead of giving it back to Vera at school, or waiting for the next time they saw each other, Aspen spontaneously showed up at Vera's house after school while Layla was, luckily, at dance class. It was a total excuse just to see her, but they ended up going to Vera's room.

Then they lost track of time. Accidentally. One moment Vera was kissing Aspen innocently, and the next Aspen had Vera pinned on the bed, straddling her waist while kissing her. All precaution flew out of Vera's head, and the only thing she could think about was Aspen's mouth on hers, and how every touch against her skin was like flint scraping on stone.

"We should stop," Aspen said breathlessly against Vera's mouth, before kissing her again.

Then they heard the door swing open downstairs, and Layla speaking loudly and laughing as if she were on the phone. Aspen pulled back abruptly, and they stared at each other.

"Shit," Aspen said.

Vera could feel her heart thumping in her chest, and her stomach twisting. They didn't need to say it. Vera saw her own thoughts reflected in Aspen's eyes. Because there were only so many times you could make excuses before someone started to catch on.

She took a deep breath and exhaled slowly. "We should go downstairs." Even though Vera dreaded the thought of facing her sister, she felt more confident with Aspen by her side.

Aspen looked at her worriedly. "Okay," she said, her voice hardly more than a whisper.

They got off the bed, Vera flattening her hair, and Aspen fixing her shorts. Then Aspen turned to Vera and grabbed her hand. "No matter what happens," Aspen said, then she kissed her quickly. Vera caught herself trying to memorize how Aspen's lips felt against her own, before she shook her head and followed Aspen down the stairs.

Vera tried to run through the possible scenarios, but her mind was frozen in terror, like a deer caught in the headlights. Her hand shook as she held onto the railing.

Why did it feel like so much was at stake right now?

Then suddenly there was Layla, grabbing something from the fridge. Aspen and Vera walked towards her slowly, and Vera wondered if it was a good idea to spring this on Layla.

"Hey Layla," Aspen said, the hesitation and awkwardness clear in her voice.

Layla whirled around, startled, her mouth parted in shock. She looked from Vera to Aspen uncomprehendingly. Vera could only imagine how they looked, both of them flushed and disheveled.

"Aspen? What's going on?" Layla asked, still looking between the two of them with a strange look. "I've tried calling you like five times."

"My phone was on silent. Why?" Aspen asked. Vera could tell she was trying to keep her voice from wavering.

Layla had her hands on her hips now. "Your mom called me. She was trying to call you because your dad was sent home today. And you know what's funny? She said that you told her you were with me." *Shit.* "Since when do you lie to your mom?"

Aspen was silent for a beat. Then, "Did you tell her the truth?"

Layla rolled her eyes impatiently. "Of course I covered

for you. I thought maybe you were with Maxwell. But then I find you here. What's going on, Aspen?"

When neither of them answered, Layla turned towards Vera. "And you. Is that a hickey on your neck?" Layla asked, disbelieving. She walked towards Vera and touched her neck with her fingertips. Vera winced, but not because it hurt.

"I'm dating your sister," Aspen said, quiet but firm. She stared straight at Layla, who slowly backed away with wide eyes. Vera looked at Aspen with the same surprise. She knew Aspen was bold, but this was different. This really mattered.

Layla huffed a laugh. "Are you serious?"

"Yes," Aspen said.

Layla crossed her arms again and looked skyward. "That's not possible." Then Layla looked at Vera, and the anger shining in her eyes nearly rocked Vera back on her heels. "Vera, tell me she's lying."

"She's not," Vera said, so softly she wasn't sure Layla even heard.

Layla gritted her teeth. "I can't believe you. Both of you." Then with a venom Vera didn't think she possessed, choked out, "Aspen, couldn't you play around with anyone else? And really, Vera? You decided to fall in love with my *best friend?*"

Layla's voice cracked at the last word, and the look of disappointment on her face struck Vera like an arrow to the heart. Somehow it was worse than anger. Then without another word, Layla spun on her heel and walked straight out the door.

Vera and Aspen remained still for what felt like an eternity after the slammed door echoed throughout the house. Then Aspen took Vera's hand.

"She'll come around," Aspen said, though she didn't sound like she believed it.

Vera's eyes welled with tears before she could stop them. She shook her head, sending tears rolling down her cheeks, before gently pushing Aspen's hand away and heading upstairs to her room.

She could hear Aspen sigh sadly before she closed the door.

14

When Vera realized she had finished getting ready for school, and there was nothing else to pack, she had to suck it up and go downstairs. She heard the clinking of cutlery in the kitchen and sighed.

With her backpack slung over her shoulder, Vera walked down the stairs. Just as she was dreading, Layla was sitting at the kitchen bar eating her breakfast cereal. Vera went into the kitchen, grabbing a bowl and spoon. Layla didn't spare her a glance, instead briskly gathering her things and heading out the door.

Well, she hadn't miraculously forgotten about Aspen and her then.

Vera checked her phone as she took a bite of her cereal. Aspen had texted her three times.

Aspen: Call me, please.

Aspen: Don't shut me out.

Aspen: I know what you're going through and I'm here when you need me.

Vera dialed Aspen's number. After a few rings, Aspen picked up.

"You called," Aspen said after a beat of silence.

"Yeah," Vera said awkwardly.

"Let's talk," Aspen pleaded.

"About what? How my sister hates me now?" Vera grimaced at the resentment in her voice. After all, hadn't Aspen also been on the receiving end of Layla's anger and disappointment? "Sorry," Vera added miserably.

Aspen ignored her tone. "Let's talk. Please."

"After school," Vera relented.

There was a sigh like Aspen wouldn't mind coming over now. She would probably skip school if Vera suggested it. "Fine. Your house?"

"No, Layla's going to be here," Vera said.

"How about the bookstore?" Aspen offered.

Vera nodded, checking the time. If they didn't leave now they would be late to school. "I have to go. But meet there after school?"

"I'll be there."

School was entirely uneventful up until lunch. Piper and Vera sat at their usual table alone since Jane was absent.

Both of them were chewing silently on their food when Will showed up, sitting down without a hello, his face in a sullen pout.

"Never thought I'd see the day you didn't have a smile on your face. Is the world coming to an end, or what?" Vera said, jokingly.

Will glared at her, then sighed. "I just saw Layla with her boyfriend."

Guess that meant Layla chose. Vera felt bad for Will. She hadn't realized how much he liked Layla. Piper sat watching the conversation unfold with rapt focus, munching on her sandwich.

"Maybe they were breaking up?" Vera offered, though she sounded doubtful.

Suddenly Aspen came and sat down at the table, a soda in hand. Will and Piper both looked startled at the new addition to the table.

"Actually, they're planning for a special night, if you catch my drift," Aspen said, taking a sip of her soda.

Vera glared at Aspen, then turned to Will with an apologetic smile. "She's just joking."

"No, I'm not," Aspen said, smirking. Vera rolled her eyes and took a bite of her apple. Will watched the interaction with equal measures of surprise and misery.

At last, Vera couldn't hold it in any longer. "Aspen,

what are you doing here?"

"Well, as you know, Layla hates me, so I don't really have a place to eat. Usually I go to the library of all places when I have to eat alone, but today I thought I would come by and surprise you." Aspen sighed dramatically and stood up. "But seeing as I'm not welcome here either, I'll just go."

Vera didn't know whether to laugh or call after her. "Wait, Aspen—"

"See you later, babe," Aspen interrupted, before sauntering off. Will looked after her in shock. Piper looked ready to burst. Vera felt her face heat up at their stares.

"Did she just call you babe?" Piper asked, her eyes wide.

"Yep," Vera said, before letting her face fall into her hands, ignoring Piper's squeal.

The bookstore was nearly empty when Vera showed up. Too anxious to look around, she sat down at one of the tables, running a hand through her hair. It wasn't long before Vera began to doubt. What if Aspen didn't show up? What if she was angry? What if—

"Vera."

Vera looked up sharply. Aspen stood on the other side

of the table. She wasn't in her school uniform anymore, instead dressed in black jeans and a bright red sweater. Vera stood up, and Aspen walked around to her side of the table.

"I didn't think you'd come," Vera said quietly, surprised at her honesty.

"I didn't think you'd be here either," Aspen confessed. She looked at Vera for a few moments—longingly, Vera realized—before Aspen stepped forward and hugged her tightly. "I'm sorry," she whispered.

Vera sighed into the embrace, secretly enjoying how, slowly, Aspen was becoming more familiar, her scent, her touch, her kiss. "I'm sorry too."

When they finally released each other, Aspen pressed a delicate kiss on Vera's lips. The effect was immediate, and Vera's hands found Aspen's waist automatically.

"I think you should try to talk with Layla," Aspen said quietly, taking one of Vera's hands in hers and threading their finger together. "She's your sister."

"I don't know…"

"If anyone can talk with her, it's you." Aspen looked down at their entwined hands. "I've tried, but I think she blocked my number."

Vera hesitated, her stomach tightening into painful knots, but then Aspen looked up, her eyes hopeful, and

Vera relented. "Okay, when I go home I'll talk with her."

Aspen smiled, and that alone made everything worth it. "Now that *that's* settled…"

"Let me guess," Vera said, rolling her eyes, "let's find a dark corner to make out?"

"You're learning," Aspen said with a smirk, before pulling Vera towards the bookshelves.

15

Vera arrived home two hours later. Her mom and dad were still at work, but they would be arriving sometime soon. That only gave Vera a little bit of time to try and talk to Layla.

She looked around as the front door closed loudly behind her. The kitchen was empty, but the living room was not. Layla was curled up on the couch with a bag of chips in her hand. The TV was playing House Hunters, a show that Layla liked to watch when she was feeling sad or lonely.

"Not hanging out with your boyfriend?" Vera asked as she walked towards the couch.

Layla glared at Vera, then turned back to the TV. But she didn't get up to leave, so Vera considered it progress. Then she said curtly, "We broke up."

"I'm sorry," Vera said.

Layla sighed, then slumped back against the couch. "I don't even know why I'm sad. We were planning to…go all the way tonight." She blushed, glancing at Vera as if to gauge her reaction. "But then we got to his house and all I could think about was Will. So I broke up with him and left."

"Oh?" Vera cautiously sat down at the other end of the couch.

"Look, I know why you're here, and it's not to comfort me," Layla said bitterly.

Even though her heart ached for her sister, it was impossible to ignore the elephant in the room. Vera sighed. "I want to talk."

"About what?" Layla demanded, as if she wanted Vera to say it out loud.

"Aspen," Vera said quietly. Layla's jaw tightened. "I'm sorry." Her voice wavered. Vera felt her eyes sting and well up, and she wiped her cheeks as the tears fell.

"Why are you crying?" Layla asked angrily, but her eyes revealed a hesitation.

Vera shook her head. "I knew you were going to be mad about Aspen, but I just thought you would still…accept me." The tears were falling faster now, and she struggled to stop.

Layla's face froze in realization, then crumbled. "Oh god. I'm so sorry Vera. I hadn't even—I was so focused on you stealing Aspen that I didn't even think. God, I'm so stupid." Layla crawled towards Vera and hugged her tightly. Vera could not help but cry into her shoulder.

"I thought you were disgusted with me," Vera whispered.

Layla smoothed Vera's back. "Of course not! I'm your sister. I love you no matter what."

When they pulled apart, Vera felt a weight rise from her shoulders. "I love you too." Layla smiled, her eyes shining, and took her hand. Vera took a shaky breath. "But I am sorry. I didn't mean for Aspen to happen. It just did. But if it really makes you upset, I'll break up with her."

"No, don't break up with her," Layla said hurriedly, then paused, her eyes not quite reaching Vera's. "But I am worried."

"Why?" Vera asked, feeling that familiar tingle of panic in her chest.

Layla bit her lip. "Well, Aspen, at least with boys…gets around. I just mean, she's been with a lot of people, and usually only for a short amount of time. I'm scared she might hurt you."

Vera glanced down. "Me too," she admitted.

"You know about Kyle? And how they ended?" Layla asked.

"Yeah, she told me," Vera said warily, worried that

there was more to the story.

Layla looked startled. "She did?"

Vera nodded. "Yeah."

"Really?" Layla looked shocked. "Even about Sydney?"

"Yeah, why is that so hard to believe?" Vera asked impatiently.

"Aspen never talks about personal stuff," Layla said.

Vera could not help but blush. "Oh."

Layla frowned, looking down at her hands, seemingly lost in thought.

"You should talk to her," Vera said gently. "Aspen loves you. A lot. And she's worried she lost her best friend." Layla stayed silent. "And I know you love her too."

Layla sighed and looked up at Vera. "Yeah, I do. I think I might find her now, if you don't mind."

Vera smiled. "Not at all."

Layla gave Vera's hand one last reassuring squeeze before getting up. She grabbed her phone and headed towards the door. "Well, I'm going to order a ride. See you later."

She reached for the doorknob, but stopped short, turning around. Vera raised a brow.

"Two things before I go," Layla said. "First, I think you should tell Mom and Dad. I'll come later so you guys can talk in private. If you need me, just call. Second—" Layla paused as if bracing herself. "—I have only one rule."

"What's that?"

"No PDA when I'm around," Layla said, crossing her arms.

Vera laughed, ignoring the blush forming on her cheeks. "I promise I won't, but with Aspen, who knows."

Layla groaned. "Oh god, you're right." She sighed. "Well, see you later. For real, now."

Then she was out the door, and the house went very quiet. Vera, emotionally spent, flopped back on the couch.

Her parents arrived thirty minutes later around seven o'clock in the evening, but dinner wasn't ready for another hour. By the time they all sat down together at the table, Vera was a nervous wreck. What if they hate her? No, hate was not the worst that could happen. It would be disappointment, that look of disgust, or even disbelief. She could almost hear her mom say it. *My daughter? No way.*

"Where's Layla?" her mom asked after a bite of pasta.

"At Aspen's house," Vera replied, trying to keep her voice steady. She noticed that her hands were shaking as she stabbed at a piece of chicken with her fork.

"Guess they're done fighting?" her dad asked, shaking his head in amusement.

"I think so," Vera said. She could barely swallow, her stomach dropping nervously, the palms of her hands sweating.

"Sweetie, are you okay?" her mom asked, peering at her.

Vera tried to smile, but she was pretty sure she failed. When was the right time? Her parents were both silent and Vera wasn't eating anything. Should she just go for it? Vera thought of Aspen, her boldness, and set down her fork and knife.

"How was school?" her mom asked worriedly.

"I have a girlfriend," Vera blurted out, then immediately shut her mouth, horrified that she had actually said it. But it was too late. Both her parents had gone completely still, her dad with a raised eyebrow, and her mom with wide eyes.

"Finally an interesting answer to that question," her dad said finally. "You're not joking, are you?" Vera shook her head, unable to speak. "Just wanted to make sure. Well, congratulations!"

She turned to her mom and was shocked to see the proud smile on her face. "I'm so glad you told us, Vera.

I had a hunch since you asked for that advice the other day. So, who's the lucky girl?"

Vera was still shocked at how quickly everything was happening. Somehow in her head the conversation never got past the part where she confessed that she liked girls. "Uh…"

"Don't be shy now! We want to know," her mom said excitedly.

"Yeah, we can't wait to meet her," her dad added.

"Well, you see—"

"She's not imaginary, is she?" her dad joked. Her mom shushed him. "Sorry," he said with an embarrassed smile.

Vera bit her lip. She hadn't anticipated that *this* was going to be the hardest part. "It's Aspen."

Silence. Maybe she should've made someone up…

"Layla's…best friend?" her mom asked hesitantly.

Vera sighed. "Yeah, I know."

Her dad coughed awkwardly. "Didn't see that one coming."

"Is Layla okay with it?" her mom asked, raising a dubious eyebrow.

Vera thought back to their conversation and smiled. "We talked."

For a moment there was a tense pause, and her mom glanced between Vera and her dad. Then she smiled at

Vera, her eyes full of warmth and love, and Vera had never felt so lucky.

"If you're happy, then we're happy," her mom said firmly.

Vera couldn't help but smile too.

Epilogue

Vera, Aspen, Layla, and Will all sat at a new cafe that had opened in downtown and was trending, at least according to Layla and Aspen. Layla had invited Will but hadn't told either Vera or Aspen what was going on between them. Vera hoped it was something good.

They had been joking around so much other people in the cafe were looking at them with annoyance. It was a refreshing lightness compared to the tense days a few weeks prior. Aspen called them the Dark Days.

It was strange, having a girlfriend. Vera assumed it was a lot like what having a boyfriend would be like, except that she had always felt more comfortable with girls than boys.

Aspen placed a hand on Vera's upper thigh and traced a light circle on her skin, bringing Vera back to reality. She blushed and stole a glance at Aspen's smirking face.

"Aspen!" Layla said sternly. "What was my number one rule?"

Aspen raised a brow, feigning confusion. "I'm sorry, I don't understand."

Layla narrowed her eyes at Vera. "You're not blushing because of the fries."

Vera smiled innocently. "Trust me, Layla, you don't want to know."

Aspen and Will laughed, while Layla's mouth fell open, apparently shocked that Vera had it in her. Vera was almost surprised as well. *Almost.*

Layla turned an accusing glare on Aspen. "What did you do with my sister?"

Aspen smirked. "I educated her."

After lunch, Vera and Aspen left Will and Layla at the cafe. Aspen had not been very discreet when she told them that she and Vera were going on a date. Vera liked that Aspen shipped Layla and Will together as well, and they left the two of them blushing.

"So, where are we going?" Vera asked once they were in the car.

Aspen briefly flashed her phone screen, which was open to Google Maps. "I'll tell you where to go." There was a strange glint in her eyes, but it was gone when

Aspen put on her seat belt.

Vera shrugged. "Okay, I trust you."

They ended up parking at a large mall. Vera asked again where they were going, but Aspen just said to follow her. They walked through the mall hand in hand. A few people glanced their way, but otherwise, no one paid them any attention.

At last, they rounded a corner and Aspen stopped. Before them was a large, pink storefront, covered in posters of women in colorful, lacy lingerie.

Aspen smirked. "Well, what do you know…"

"No way you brought us here," Vera said warily, eyeing the nearly naked women. She glanced around to see if anyone from school was around. This was mortifying. "I should never have trusted you."

Aspen laughed. "Hey! You were the one that suggested it."

"That was a joke!" Vera protested, covering her face with her hands.

Aspen pried them away, kissing her quickly. "Don't worry, it'll be fun!" Then she dragged Vera inside.

After a seemingly endless hour of sifting through piles and racks of different styles and colors of lingerie, Aspen finally announced that they had enough for her to try on.

"Wait, I'm trying those things on here?" Vera whispered.

Aspen looked at her strangely. "You can't just take random ones home. How will you know if they even look good?"

Vera had no good argument against it. Grudgingly, Vera followed her to the changing rooms. After all, she wouldn't want to waste money on something that didn't fit.

A woman working there led Vera to a changing room. Aspen waited in the chair outside.

Once inside, Vera picked up a black lace one piece, which was a very short dress, if dresses were entirely see-through, and read the tag. "Babydoll?" she muttered in exasperation. She thought she heard a stifled laugh on the other side of the door. Vera decidedly rummaged for the black bra and panty set they had chosen and slipped them on first, shaking her head.

But when she looked into the mirror, Vera went very still. The lingerie indeed complemented her figure, accentuating her slight curves and long legs. Vera hardly recognized the person staring back at her, the body that she had always dismissed, even disliked. It made her wonder if Aspen saw her like this. It made her wonder what Aspen would say—what she would do—if she saw Vera like this.

After she tried on the rest of the lingerie, Vera walked outside of the changing room and met Aspen.

"Well?" Aspen asked. "How did they fit?"

"I didn't really like any of them," Vera said. "I'm sorry."

Aspen looked slightly disappointed, but then smiled brightly. "That's okay. Besides, I like you best without any clothes at all."

"Hey!"

"Joking, joking," Aspen said, but her smirk suggested otherwise.

Vera drove them to her house, as Layla was still out with Will and her parents wouldn't be home until the evening. She took Aspen's hand and led her upstairs to her room.

They began to kiss. Aspen smiled against her mouth. She liked it when Vera initiated, and that made Vera like her even more. When Vera felt the room heat up, she leaned back and pulled her shirt off.

Aspen's eyes widened. "Vera," she said, breathless.

Vera looked down at her sheer black bra. It was entirely see-through. "Surprise," she said quietly, blushing.

"What? How? When?" Aspen couldn't tear her eyes away.

"I bought it a while ago," Vera admitted. "I was going to surprise you tonight."

Aspen leaned forward and kissed her. "It was certainly a surprise."

"I have an even better one waiting for you," Vera whispered, bringing Aspen's hands to her waistband and raising a brow.

"Well, well, well, Vera," Aspen said. "You are full of surprises today."

Then she pulled Vera in for another kiss.

FIVE MONTHS LATER

The August heat warmed Vera's skin as she walked up the grassy hill, glancing uneasily at the tall trees surrounding her. If she ignored the parking lot behind her, the nature park felt almost entirely removed from city life.

"Aspen, I'm here," Vera said, holding the phone up to her ear. "I just parked. Where are you?"

Aspen had given Vera loose directions to this "surprise" yesterday. Vera still had no idea why. *Maybe she's going to break up with you…*Even after all this time, some of the doubts still nagged at her. It was especially hard not to feel anxious when she was leaving for college in a month, and Aspen was going to be a senior at Hilltop High. But Vera pushed the thoughts away. The scenery was far too romantic for a break-up.

Besides, Vera had been accepted by UCLA to study engineering, which was less than an hour's drive from home. It worked for her relationship with Aspen, as well as her family, whom she wanted to stay close to.

Regardless, it still put a strain on her relationship with Aspen, as they wouldn't be able to see each other every day after school. But if they made it through this coming year, Vera planned to rent an apartment with Aspen, somewhere close to UCLA, since Aspen also wanted to move to Los Angeles and pursue modeling, which has always been her dream.

It was not a bad plan, but Vera knew that plans didn't always work out the way you expected them to.

"Just keep walking, find the dirt path," Aspen said, "and then when you reach the sign that says 'Off Trail,' turn left past the trees and into the clearing. You'll find it."

"Off trail? That sounds promising," Vera muttered. While she enjoyed nature, Vera preferred manicured gardens and trimmed trees in a pretty landscape over rough and wild terrain. And when she reached the sign and passed the trees, Vera sighed. A rough dirt path picked a narrow, root-filled trail snaking between the trees.

"It's not that bad," Aspen said, clearly amused.

Vera looked at the trees crowded together, and the weedy, wild grass. "It's pretty bad, Aspen. Are there rattlesnakes here?"

"I only saw two," Aspen said casually.

"What?!"

Aspen was laughing. "Relax, I'm joking."

"Not funny." But Vera stepped onto the path anyway.

She walked through the trees, dodging branches that stuck out like sharp needles and avoiding anything on the ground that looked like a hole or nest. Finally, she reached the edge of the trees and entered a lovely grass clearing sprinkled with colorful flowers. And in the middle of it was Aspen, sitting on a red checkered picnic blanket, with a basket and a bouquet of roses resting beside her.

Vera hung up and walked over. "What's all this?"

Aspen blushed, then grabbed the bouquet, handing it to Vera. "Happy five-month anniversary."

"I wish you would have told me we were celebrating this!" Vera exclaimed, sitting down beside her. "I would've gotten you a present."

"I wanted to surprise you," Aspen said, grinning. "Besides, you being here is a gift in itself."

Vera blushed. "That was cheesy. But thank you. You're amazing, you know that right?"

"Now I do," Aspen said as she pulled Vera in for a kiss. Without fail, Vera's stomach dropped, and her head spun. Aspen melted against her, sighing into Vera's touch. She pulled away. "We'll finish that later. But first, let's eat."

Aspen brought the picnic basket in the middle of them. She opened the lid and took out two large plastic containers. One was filled to the brim with cut-up pieces of watermelon, while the other had triangular, homemade cucumber sandwiches.

"My mom made all of this by the way," Aspen said offhandedly, though she glanced quickly at Vera to see her reaction. "She insisted."

Vera understood. Mrs. Silva wanted to make up for how she had reacted when they first told her that they were dating. It had been a hard week for Aspen's family at the time; her dad had been sent back to the hospital after another cancer scare, and her mom had been freaking out. Aspen hadn't wanted to drop the news that she had a girlfriend, but she did accidentally.

Then her mom got upset and yelled at Aspen that it wasn't the time to mess around and stress out her father while he was sick. Of course, later her mom apologized, and ever since she had been trying to make up for it.

Vera thought that Aspen was still somewhat traumatized from it, but it has been much better now. Aspen even brought Vera over for dinner, and Vera did the same. Recently Will had also brought Vera over for dinner. She had met his two moms, and they had greeted her warmly. Actually seeing their family dynamic work so well reassured Vera in ways that she had not anticipated.

When Vera and Aspen finished eating some of the sandwiches and most of the watermelon, along with refreshing cups of lemonade, it was already sunset. They cuddled close together on the blanket, their legs tangled, the sun disappearing behind the line of trees in brilliant streaks of gold and red, gradually giving way to a twilight sky glittering with stars.

Aspen draped her arm over Vera's waist, and Vera placed a hand gently against Aspen's cheek. They kissed, and it was like fireworks deep in the night, heard rather than seen. Vera moved away, kissing Aspen's jaw, her neck, and then rested her forehead against Aspen's.

They looked into each other's eyes, and Vera smiled. Aspen smiled too, her lashes fluttering over her warm gaze. She traced the outline of Vera's face with her fingertips.

"I love you," Aspen said softly. "So much."

"I love you too," Vera said, and she let Aspen pull her in again, as she had done from the very start.

Bonus Chapter 1

"Do you want to go to a party tomorrow night?" Kyle asked. Aspen glanced up at her boyfriend with feigned interest.

"I guess. Why not?"

Aspen knew full well what parties entailed when it came to Kyle. Mix alcohol and music with Kyle and he became very aggressive and excited. He was a good kisser, she gave him that, but he just didn't quite do it for her anymore.

"Do you not want to go?" Kyle asked, clearly perplexed. Aspen pacified him with one of her dazzling smiles.

"Of course I want to go. I'll drive there with Layla from her house," Aspen said. Kyle nodded, seemingly satisfied.

She wasn't exactly lying. She did want to go, at least to the first leg of the drive. Because even if she would never admit it out loud, Aspen knew she only said yes for the chance to see the one person who got her pulse racing.

Layla's older sister.

Vera.

Aspen had always sort of known. Since her first kiss with a boy, since her first party with all the girls dressed in short skirts and glossy lipstick, Aspen knew that she found both boys and girls attractive.

She also knew not everyone felt like this.

But she was fine with that. Aspen enjoyed being different, and standing out. She quickly realized, though, that being bisexual wasn't like having a pretty face or blue eyes or being fluent in Spanish. In other words, it wasn't simply a trait she had along with everything else. It was a label, something that stuck with you and defined you before you could even speak.

That's why she didn't really tell people. And because she didn't think it was anyone's business. Plus, she had a boyfriend. So what was the use in outing herself?

Then she thought of Vera.

"Daydreaming about Kyle again?" Layla teased. Aspen rolled her eyes. The one person she actually feared telling was Layla. She had been her best friend for years, but even Aspen was scared of losing a friendship if Layla didn't accept her.

"I'm just tired," Aspen lied. How could she be tired when Vera was leaning against the kitchen counter only a few feet away, one hand holding a book and the other mindlessly twisting a strand of her hair?

Aspen had first noticed Vera the summer after freshman year. Layla had invited her to join their family vacation to Palm Springs where they could swim and tan by the pool. Aspen had happily taken up the offer, eager to try on the new red bikini she had bought the week before.

They had been lounging on the pool chairs under the shade of an umbrella, sipping some iced lemonade, when Vera walked outside.

Aspen nearly dropped her glass.

Vera had long, lanky legs and a delicious olive tan. And she must have cut her hair recently because Aspen had never seen that much of Vera's chest. At that moment, it just clicked.

Since that day, every time Aspen saw Vera, her heart skipped a beat in her chest and a deep ache formed inside her.

Because if there was one person in the entire universe that she couldn't have, it was Vera.

"Are you okay?" Kyle asked when they were alone in the kitchen. Aspen had been unusually quiet all night. "Let's go upstairs, I'll make you feel better. Jack's parents are out of town."

"Why are you so horny all the time?" Aspen snapped. She was sick of him hanging around her when she knew he only wanted one thing. "Go find one of your friends and kiss him if you want to so badly."

Kyle muttered an insult under his breath and stormed off, disappearing down the hall. Aspen didn't care if this caused him to break up with her. She'd had enough of boys for one night.

"You look tense."

Aspen looked up—and saw one of the prettiest girls she had ever seen. Her brown hair was cut in a neat bob that fell just past her jaw. She wore gold hoop earrings that matched the strapless gold-yellow dress she had on, the hem falling just above her tanned legs. Her light grey eyes looked at Aspen in amusement.

"Who are you?" Aspen asked rudely, still a bit put off by Kyle and the fact that this girl looked so much like Vera.

"Sydney," the girl said warmly, stretching out a hand.

Aspen raised a brow and shook it. She knew vaguely that a certain Sydney went to their school and dated Jack, the quarterback, and whose house they were currently in. "Aspen."

"Cool name," Sydney said. She looked around then moved closer to Aspen as if she were about to tell a secret. "Boy troubles? I understand."

Aspen's nodded quickly. "It's like sometimes he only wants...you know…" She made a gesture, and Sydney giggled.

"I know what you mean," Sydney said. "They get all the fun and we have to do all the work."

"Exactly!" Aspen exclaimed, feeling elated that someone else finally understood.

Then Sydney lowered her eyelids, and Aspen's breath caught in her throat. "Maybe us girls would have more fun by ourselves."

Aspen's voice came out breathless. "Maybe we would."

Sydney tilted her head, her eyes narrowing on Aspen. "I've always wanted to try. Have you?"

Was this really happening?

"Yes," Aspen whispered.

She could barely move. It turned out she didn't have to. Sydney inched closer. Aspen looked around, only now noticing that they were alone in the kitchen. One kiss wouldn't hurt…

Sydney closed the gap. Her mouth tasted like alcohol

and lemonade, and it was warm and sure against Aspen's.

Yes. This was right. Aspen snaked her arms around Sydney, her heart thrumming in her chest at the feel of sharp hip bones and a soft waist. It was intoxicating. It was dangerous. But it was everything she had wanted and had never been able to put into words.

"Aspen!?"

"Sydney?"

Shit.

She didn't know how she got here. One minute she was downing her first shot of the night, trying to forget about Kyle and Sydney and everything else, and the next minute she was standing in front of *her* house.

Aspen's knuckles rasped against the familiar wooden door. After a few minutes of the world swinging around her, the door opened, with Vera on the other side.

Oh my. Aspen barely held back a gasp. She was stunning. Okay, maybe not red carpet stunning in those sweatpants and messy hair, but she was still gorgeous to Aspen, who could not stop staring at the beautiful face hiding behind her red-framed glasses. She nearly swooned right then and there.

"Aspen?"

Aspen wanted to say something but her stomach lurched with the different alcohols she had consumed, and she teetered to the side.

"What are you doing here?" Vera asked, more worriedly this time.

Vera's body doubled then blurred, and suddenly Aspen lost balance and pitched forward, landing heavily in Vera's arms. Her head spun and she struggled to stand up straight.

"I'm so drunk right now," Aspen said, giggling at how her voice sounded.

Vera had gone deathly still, her hair barely moving against Aspen's cheek.

"You're pretty," Aspen said, marveling at Vera's olive skin, all shiny and smooth. It was the same skin that she kissed over and over again in all her fantasies at night, and she had to restrain herself from kissing it now.

"Maybe you should lie down," Vera suggested awkwardly. She dragged Aspen to the couch, and Aspen clumsily sank into the cushions.

Something turned in her stomach at the movement, and a painful wave of nausea rose up her throat.

"I think I'm going to throw up," Aspen mumbled.

Vera's eyes widened, before she dashed to the kitchen.

Aspen had the fleeting fear that Vera had abandoned her, but it disappeared when Vera returned, bowl in hand.

When Aspen's hands cupped the bowl, vomit rose up her throat uncontrollably, stinging her nose. Aspen gurgled, trying not to throw up again, and spat the acidic fluid out of her mouth. Only when she finished did Aspen realize that Vera had pulled back her hair with her hands.

"Sorry," Aspen muttered, feeling humiliated. Vera gently lowered her hair from her grasp.

"It's okay," Vera said. She took the bowl and went to the bathroom, flushing the contents, then back to the kitchen.

Now that Aspen had vomited, she felt marginally better. Her vision was more or less normal now, and she wasn't quite so dizzy, though she still felt very drunk.

Vera came back with a cleaned bowl, tucking a strand of her short brown hair behind her ear. "Just in case you need it again."

Aspen tried to smile, looking anywhere but those green eyes. "Thank you." She thought that Vera would walk away, but when she didn't, her heart swooped in her chest.

"Do you want to talk?" Vera asked hesitantly.

Aspen's gaze snapped up, startled. Her heart thrashed against her ribs, and she frowned at the intensity of her emotions. This couldn't happen, not now and not ever.

This was Layla's *sister.*

"I'm really tired. Do you think I could crash here for the night?" Aspen asked. Vera hesitated, and Aspen wondered if she had been rude.

"Sure. You can sleep in Layla's room. She's in San Diego." Vera sounded slightly disheartened, but maybe that was just Aspen's wishful thinking.

"I know," Aspen said without realizing.

"Right," Vera said stiffly. The awkwardness of it all nearly sobered Aspen up completely.

Suddenly, Vera reached out her hand. Aspen blinked at it, unsure what was happening. Vera grabbed the bowl with one hand and with the other hand she helped Aspen stand up.

"Come on, I'll help you upstairs," Vera said.

Aspen nodded, holding her hand tightly. She stood up, then immediately lost balance. Vera placed a delicate hand on the small of her back, and a rush of electricity exploded where her skin touched the thin fabric of Aspen's dress. If anything, Vera was making her more dizzy.

By the time they made it to Layla's room, Aspen's head was heavy and her limbs ached. Thankfully the room was dark, and the bed invitingly empty. Aspen sat down on the edge of the bed, pulled her heels off, and then crawled into the soft sheets, enveloping herself in the familiarity of them.

Vera's presence was still hovering. A surge of gratitude flooded through Aspen.

"Thank you. Again," Aspen said.

"It was no problem. Really." Vera smiled kindly and then left, closing the door softly behind her.

In the pitch black, all Aspen had to do was give in to the exhaustion and she fell into a deep, hazy sleep. After what seemed like hours, she felt Vera's presence again, but at first she thought it was a dream. She heard the sound of glass placed on wood and near-silent breaths coming from somewhere to her right. Her legs were cold, and she wondered where the blankets had gone. How much time had passed?

Aspen twisted around, trying to find the blankets, reluctantly blinking her eyes open, only to see Vera frozen at the edge of the bed, eyes trained on her legs. Her dress must've ridden up while she was sleeping.

Before Vera could see that she was awake, Aspen closed her eyes again. The floorboards creaked from the weight of footsteps, and then blankets tickled the sides of Aspen's legs, and the sheets were once again over her body. Aspen could hear the soft breaths Vera made as she stepped back. She should say something. Aspen heard a hand turning the door knob.

"Vera?" Aspen asked, hating the sound of her voice, all groggy and weak. She turned and squinted at her in the dark.

Vera didn't say anything, standing at the door with a look half of surprise, half of embarrassment, her hand still on the doorknob.

"Please don't tell Layla I was here," Aspen said, not realizing that was what she wanted to say until she had said it aloud. A part of her felt ashamed that the one time they were alone together, Vera had to see her like this. She wondered what Vera thought of her, and what she would think if she knew what Aspen had done tonight.

"I won't," Vera said quietly. She held her gaze for a moment more, before fleeing the room.

When she was gone, Aspen let out a long sigh. She spotted the ibuprofen and water, and it got her heart pounding so fast she was scared it would burst. After downing the pills, Aspen closed her eyes again, hoping to get a few more good hours of sleep before she left.

As she fell asleep once more, Aspen only hoped that after tonight she would have the good sense to stay away.

But she never did have good sense, did she?

Bonus Chapter 2

spen stared at the ceiling. She rolled onto her stomach, adjusting the pillow under her chin. Her mind couldn't stop replaying the past hours, Vera's hand curling behind her neck, gentle fingers playing with her hair. Even with a bookshelf digging into her back, all she could feel were Vera's soft lips on hers, the curve of Vera's waist against her arm.

But she also couldn't deny the small voice in the back of her mind, worrying about Layla, her best friend, and how her conversation with Vera was going. Could it be that she'll lose both Layla *and* Vera?

Knock knock knock.

Aspen's head snapped up. Her first thought was Vera. But she wouldn't show up without texting first. Could it be...Layla? Or a false alarm?

The knocks came again, harder this time. Aspen got up and quickly went downstairs, throwing open the front door.

Layla stood on the porch with a guarded expression, her hands fiddling with her phone. Aspen stared, unsure of what to say.

"Can we talk?" Layla asked.

Aspen nodded silently, too shocked to say anything.

Layla followed her inside, the tension hanging over them like a thick fog.

"What do you want to talk about?" Aspen asked uneasily. She knew exactly what Layla wanted to talk about. Vera. But that only made her nerves spike higher.

Aspen sat on the couch. Layla took a seat on the chair in front of her, shifting uncomfortably and avoiding her gaze.

"Look, Aspen, I talked with Vera," Layla said, and Aspen held her breath, "and she really cares for you. Clearly she sees a lot of *something* in you, otherwise this wouldn't be happening. And I know that you're a good person. But as much as I love you, Vera's my sister, and I don't want to see her getting hurt."

Aspen swallowed. "I don't know what to say in order to reassure you. Vera…" Her image floated in Aspen's mind easily: short brown hair, bright green eyes behind red frames, but most of all the essence of her, the confident, contained way she held herself, the smile she had when talking about the things she loved. "She's too good for me. I know that."

Layla frowned, her eyes troubled. "Aspen….you do realize how hard it is for me, right? I see how you are with the boys you supposedly like. What else am I supposed to think?"

Aspen knew too well what Layla saw, and ever since she started to really *see* Vera, Aspen had desperately wanted to change.

"Don't you think I know that? Vera's so smart, kindhearted, and focused on her goals. The opposite of me. Don't you think I know that she'll wake up one day and realize that I'm not worth it? Don't you think I know that every day when she texts me goodnight, I'm just so lucky to have even the slightest bit of her attention, to be in her life like that for one more day?"

Layla's mouth was parted in surprise. "Aspen, I'm not saying you're not worth it. Of course you are. It's just, this is my *sister*."

"I didn't mean for it to happen, okay?" Aspen said defensively.

"You have to promise me, then, that you won't hurt her. Because if you do, I don't know what I'll do," Layla said, her eyes hardening resolutely. Aspen bit her lip. "And I don't mean breaking up," Layla added, "because that's not something you can control. I'm talking about getting bored of her and then dumping her like you did with all your exes."

Aspen winced. "She's not like that. Vera's different." It sounded childish, even to Aspen. Layla rubbed her temples, clearly distressed.

"Will this ever not get weird?" Layla wondered aloud.

"I'm still your best friend," Aspen said softly.

Layla's eyebrows raised, and a crooked smile appeared on her lips. "And I'm still yours. But I'm not going to sit back and let you take advantage of my sister if I can stop it. Because Vera doesn't take these things lightly."

"I don't take them lightly either," Aspen countered, then adding when Layla gave her a look, "*anymore*. Vera gets me. I'm like an open book around her, and all the walls I put up just fall down. What else am I supposed to do? I've never felt like this before with anyone else. I can't just let her get away."

Layla scrutinized Aspen's face. Eventually, she relaxed with a frown, giving up. "Okay. I believe you. But don't think for a second that this changes the fact that I *will* destroy you if anything happens to her."

And Aspen believed her. Besides, she knew it was pointless to argue, because Layla would never understand that it wasn't Vera who needed protection, but *her*. Aspen was allowing her heart to be explored by someone who actually cared, and who could spear a knife through it with just a single word. She never had to be vulnerable like this before, and it terrified and compelled her at the same time, like standing at the edge of a cliff causes both fear and fascination.

"I know," Aspen said with half a smile. "And I would let you."

Layla held out her pinky. "Pinky swear."

Aspen knew the gravity of such a promise. She linked their fingers together, locking eyes with Layla. "Pinky swear."

When they sat back, Layla smiled brightly. Aspen relaxed, relief coursing through her.

"Now that that's over, let's talk. So, have you taken her on a date?" Layla asked. Aspen blanched.

"W-what? I thought—" Aspen stuttered, thrown off by the question.

Layla raised a concerned eyebrow. "Aspen, babe, I may be Vera's sister, but I'm also your best friend. And right now, you need a best friend." She crossed her arms, daring Aspen to challenge her logic.

Aspen shook her head. "You're amazing."

"I know," Layla quipped, before attacking Aspen with a million questions.

And despite how awkward it still felt, Aspen had never

been more grateful that Layla was her best friend.

Sneak Peek into the Sequel:

Best Friends & Their Exes

1

"Are you sure you don't want to come with us?" Jenny asked.

Aspen looked up at Jenny and tried to smile. "I'm busy, but maybe next week."

"You say that every time," Jenny said with a sigh. "But your call."

Her other colleagues said their goodbyes and began filing out of the studio. Jenny flipped her bleach-dyed blonde hair behind her shoulder and walked out the door with the rest of the model agency staff. Except Aspen.

"I'll close up," Aspen called after them, even though they already knew she would.

Once they were all out the door, Aspen sighed, running a hand through her hair. She itched to get out her phone and text Vera, to ask her to come over or something since it was a Friday night. But she knew Vera wouldn't answer, and even if she did, she would say that she was studying and didn't want any distractions. That's all Aspen was to her now—a distraction.

Her time so far in Los Angeles hadn't been what she expected. She had thought they would take on the glitz and glam together, holding hands and daring anyone to judge them for it. Aspen had thought she would be a famous model by now and Vera would study at UCLA and they would have fun together at college parties.

Instead, Aspen was a struggling model, working an underpaid assistant job at an agency to pay the rent for her expensive apartment, while Vera studied at UCLA and never had time for her. Aspen didn't blame Vera for studying a lot and caring about her grades. But even when she wasn't in class or preparing for a big exam, if Aspen asked whether she wanted to come over, Vera claimed she was too tired, or that she was meeting with a classmate to study, or she had to visit her family. There was always an excuse.

Aspen hadn't brought up her concerns with Vera yet because she was scared of losing her again. The first time was horrible, even though it wasn't technically a breakup. At the beginning of her senior year, they 'took time off' because Vera's schedule was too busy, what with adjusting to UCLA's heavy workload and the long distance putting a strain on their relationship. In other words, they were breaking up. Aspen had cried for three days straight after that and had missed a week of school.

The rest of senior year was miserable. Aspen tried to be happy, to think of the good things in her life, like her dad being cancer-free and the family adopting another dog, but it just wasn't the same. Layla had even suggested seeing a therapist.

And then the summer came, Vera along with it. They started hanging out again, and soon enough they were back to where they started a year ago. At the time, Aspen had been excited and hopeful about the upcoming year, about living in Los Angeles and sharing an apartment with Vera.

But two months into the Fall semester, Aspen realized that things had changed. Instead of sharing an apartment together, Vera had opted to live in UCLA housing with her freshman-year roommate, claiming that it was cheaper and more convenient, despite the fact that she had always complained about the small rooms and her roommate's messy habits. Though she promised that they would move in together next year, Vera was completely engrossed in her studies and her engineering friends, and she seemed to be losing interest in Aspen as well.

Now Aspen was just waiting for Vera to finally end it.

After thirty minutes of driving solemnly from the agency, Aspen arrived at her apartment. She tried not to think too hard about the loneliness she felt upon being greeted by darkness, with no signs of life save for her pet fish on the side table.

It was almost ten o'clock at night, so she decided to text Vera.

Aspen: *Have a good day?*

Aspen was surprised when Vera answered a few seconds later.

Vera: *Not really…*

Aspen: *Want me to come over?*

Vera: *Only if you want to.*

Aspen stared at her screen in shock. This must've been the first time in weeks that Vera let her come over to her dorm. Her hands trembled as she typed a reply.

Aspen: *Be there in ten.*

She grabbed her keys again and jogged outside. It was hard not to speed, but Aspen restrained herself so that she wouldn't risk a speeding ticket. After ten long minutes, she finally reached UCLA and entered the parking lot near Vera's dorm. It was at least a two-minute walk, but she didn't mind as long as she got to see Vera.

The door to the dorm lobby opened, revealing Vera's familiar red glasses and frizzy, brown hair that she had always found endearing. Aspen could tell how exhausted she was in her lackluster smile.

"Hey," Vera said quietly as she opened the door wider for Aspen to come inside.

Aspen took her hand and kissed her briefly. "It's good to see you."

Vera averted her eyes and led them to her dorm room on the first floor. "My roommate isn't here yet."

They silently entered her dorm room, a small space hardly wide enough to have two twin beds placed on either side. Vera's roommate was messy and her bed was covered in dirty laundry and textbooks. Vera's side, on the other hand, was impeccable, her bed made with a pastel striped duvet and her books neatly stacked on her desk.

Aspen laced their hands together as they sat on the edge of the small bed. "So tell me. What's going on?"

"I'm just exhausted," Vera said, looking at her lap, "and I haven't had more than ten hours of sleep this entire week."

Aspen inspected Vera more closely and was mildly horrified at the dark smudges under Vera's eyes, the cracked lips, and the paleness of her complexion. "That's awful! You won't be able to survive the whole year if you keep that up. You shouldn't have so much work to do that you can't get at least four or five hours of sleep a night. It's inhumane."

Vera pulled her hand away to fix her glasses and smooth down her hair. "I would be able to get more hours of sleep if my dorm building ever slept at night. All they do is party and play loud music. Even if I do get work done early, I can never fall asleep. Like, don't they have lives?"

Aspen didn't hesitate. "You can move in with me," she offered, trying to tone down her excitement. Vera immediately shrunk away from her, like Aspen knew she would, avoiding Aspen's eyes.

"I don't know—"

"But I know," Aspen interrupted.

Vera picked at the threads of the mattress. "I think—"

"Don't think."

"But—" Vera started.

"What are you so scared of?"

Vera exhaled, clearly vexed. "Aspen…"

Aspen groaned. "It would be perfect! You'd have a quiet place to work, and UCLA is only ten minutes away. And on the weekends we could go to parties if you were free or spend all day inside if we wanted."

But Vera looked unconvinced. "That's a little…fast, don't you think?"

"Vera, we've been together for almost two years," Aspen said, watching as Vera blushed and turned away uncomfortably. "Wait, you're not worried about...the intimacy part, are you? Because I feel like we've covered a fair share of ground on that front."

Vera blushed a darker shade of red. "No."

"Then what is it? I just don't get it. Do you even like me anymore?" Aspen was only half-serious, but Vera's head shot up, and the sparkling guilt in her eyes was answer enough. Aspen stood up from the bed, her face hot with embarrassment.

"I should go," Aspen said, numbly heading toward the door. "Clearly you don't even want to be with me."

"Aspen, wait," Vera said warily. Aspen paused with her hand on the doorknob. "I didn't say that. But aren't you worried it's not going to work out? You're busy with modeling, I'm busy with school. Maybe it's not meant to be. We tried to make it work but…"

"But that's life, Vera," Aspen said angrily, turning around. "We'll always be busy. *You're* the one who never makes the time for us anymore. I never go to parties with my colleagues because of us. I live alone in my sad, dark apartment because of you. We never do any fun things because *you* always have an excuse."

Vera's eyes filled with tears as Aspen spoke, but she found it hard to care when Vera was the one who was having doubts in the first place. "Well, maybe you *should* go party with your model friends. Maybe that way you'll find a hotter replacement for me and you can finally have all the fun you want without me dampening your mood."

"Oh, that's rich coming from you. You're the one who constantly hangs out with your engineering friends instead of your girlfriend! Am I not smart enough for you or something?"

Before Vera could answer, the door swung open. Vera's roommate walked inside, eyeing Vera and Aspen curiously as she dumped her backpack on her desk and crawled into her bed, immediately scrolling on her phone.

"You should go," Vera said quietly, remaining on the bed, a tear sliding down her cheek. "I have class early tomorrow morning."

Aspen hesitated, but when she saw Vera's stiff posture and the resolution in her eyes, she knew the argument would go nowhere. She practically ran back to her car, and only once she entered her apartment did she allow herself to collapse on her bed and cry.

When her tears subsided, Aspen grabbed her phone. Vera hadn't even tried to text or call. Aspen dialed the number of the one person whom she could talk with, who understood how much Vera meant to her.

"Aspen?" Layla said when the line connected. Aspen

hiccuped before she could say anything. "Aspen, what's wrong?"

The tears started to fall rapidly again. Her voice was thick and wavering when she said, "It's over."

Layla sucked in a breath on the other end of the line. "Are you—did she end it?"

Aspen sobbed again, louder and more pitiful. "B-basically."

"But what did she say?" Layla pressed.

"She said…she said that I should go party with my model friends, that we tried to make it work but we're too busy," Aspen said, then took in a deep breath. "I don't want to talk about it."

"Okay, you don't have to. I'll talk with her," Layla said hurriedly. "It'll be alright, Aspen. I promise."

But Aspen didn't believe her. Because without Vera, her life was empty and pointless. Nothing could ever be alright again.

Acknowledgements

First and foremost, I would like to thank all of my readers on Wattpad who read this story in its earliest conception and who left likes and comments along the way. Your support of this story, however simple and cliché it is, gave me the confidence to pursue writing as a career.

Second of all, thank you to my family, who has always been so supportive of my storytelling dreams. Your encouragement and love has been and forever will be so important to me.

Lastly, I would like to thank my younger self, who wrote this story at a time when she was just beginning to know herself. This story gave her hope, and now, perhaps, it will give hope to you too.

About the Author

Zoë Tavares Bennett is a writer based in Los Angeles, California. She is the author of the YA novel *My Sister's Best Friend* and the ancient historical retelling, *The Sun of God*. She has a degree in Classics from Williams College, specializing in Ancient Greek and Latin.

www.ingramcontent.com/pod-product-compliance
Lightning Source LLC
Chambersburg PA
CBHW061542310726
48972CB00008B/2571